CHOICE OF THE TRAVELER

MORE BOOKS BY TONI BINNS

Nexus Universe - Traveler Series

- Traveler Forgotten (*Short Story*) - Available at tonibinns.com
- Choice of the Traveler
- Call of the Traveler

CHOICE OF THE TRAVELER

TRAVELER

BOOK ONE

TONI BINNS

BARDHWOOD PRESS, LLC

Published by Bardhwood Press, LLC, Shelton, WA

Paperback ISBN: 979-8-9853073-0-6

Library of Congress Control Number: 2022923974

To all the dreamers, and those who want to read those dreams.

CHAPTER ONE

"Fake it 'till you make it," Betha whispered to herself, blinking her hazel eyes to keep the tears at bay. Worry and concern about her mother crept to the front of her mind, even as she tried to push it back. Thankfully, she wasn't driving. The taxi driver was the one navigating the roads away from the long-term care facility. She ignored the looks pointed her way in the rearview mirror and kept her eyes on the passing scenery. The view outside her window changed slowly from buildings nestled next to each other separated only by alleys to more open, green spaces with lawns and trees. From the city to the country, but not to the loved—yet rundown—part of town she used to live in. No, never again, as much as that hurt. Betha brushed her brown hair out of her eyes. She kept herself focused on her own thoughts and what was outside her window as the slight nausea of motion sickness came and went. The back seat had never been her favorite place to ride. The sign announcing that they were passing into Pack lands soothed her stomach; it wouldn't be long now. They were almost there.

The silence in the car had survived the entire trip, turning awkward by the time the taxi pulled over toward the sidewalk underneath a big tree. Betha tried to smile as she opened the door into the sunshine. The driver was already setting her duffle bag and suitcase on the sidewalk when she got out of the car.

"How much do I owe you?" she asked, pulling out her wallet.

The older gentleman gave her a soft smile. "Don't worry about it. Focus on moving in." He slammed the trunk closed and then he was off before Betha could object. Her shock left her mouth hanging open, stunned for a moment that he had just driven nearly an hour without being paid. Sure, he had picked her up at Luna's Grace with everything she owned, but did she really seem so lost, even to a total stranger?

"Fake it 'till you make it," Betha said to herself again before she snapped her mouth shut and glanced around to see where she needed to go next. It was move-in day, and she should be happy. This dorm block shouldn't be as busy, since it was for the older students. Yet people were milling about, carrying boxes and bags, and she felt thoroughly out of place. The brick buildings that lined the courtyard and tall trees made the area feel older. Picnic tables already had students at them with boxes stacked up. Everything was so open, well-kept, and *nice.*

It took a moment, but she slowly realized that almost all the students were Others. Little things began to stick out, like people carrying way more than they should, pointed ears, and even some abnormal skin colors, like green. This was going to be something she needed to get used to.

Betha had spent her first two years at the local community college full of ungifted humans. Only a few Others attended to get cheap prerequisites done. And now here she was at the opposite end of the spectrum, at one of the most prestigious Other-focused universities in the state. It was interesting what an hour-long drive could change. One area was a human centric town by choice, and here she was on Pack land. Her stomach twisted, as she could see how normal she seemed compared to the rest of them. Normal in the human sense—she didn't have pointed ears or a bright skin tone. Instead, her main feature was her piercing hazel eyes. All the doubts of transferring to this school, and selling the house to pay for it, hit her hard. The house she had grown up in, that she and her mom had shared as adults these past few years, was now gone forever.

"Fake it 'till you make it," she whispered to herself a third time. The mantra was to keep her from worrying. It wasn't really working, but it was all she had. She was here to learn everything she could about business. Her goal was to eventually own a little café, maybe even buy the coffee shop downtown that she used to work at. Christy, the owner, would be retiring in a few years. If she could get her degree, and find someone willing to back her, it was possible.

"Betha!"

Betha turned toward the sound, recognizing that voice instantly. It was one reason she was at this school to begin with. She smiled with what felt like the first true smile in a long time as her eyes locked with her best friend, Angie. Those bright golden eyes were recognizable, especially when framed by Angie's long, dark hair. Betha couldn't help but laugh as Angie darted across the pavement, dodging the shifters and elves, and whatever else tried to mow her down, without seeming to break a sweat. It was almost like a dance until she almost ran straight into a guy who must have been a troll. He towered above Angie, with two horns coming out of his forehead and his skin a deep green. "Sorry!" Angie yelled, as she moved quicker than Betha could keep track of to get out of the way.

"You are finally here in the big league! The college of Saint Luna for the win! I told you that you'd get into the swankiest school realm-side!" Angie announced as she finally stood next to her friend. Betha gave in to the hug as Angie pulled her forward, and she felt like it would all work out. It was enough to ground her and let her push the doubts about being here to the back of her mind. The height difference between the two of them always made her feel like a little sister in the best way possible.

"It is sooo good to see you. This morning kinda sucked," she whispered into Angie's hair.

"Aw!" Angie gave her a tighter squeeze. "You did the right thing. You couldn't keep taking care of your mom. She would want this for you."

"I know." Betha sniffled. "She would push me out the door to figure out who I am."

Angie rubbed her back. "Your mom was the best, and

now she is in a really great place where they can take care of her."

"Angie, you coming?" said a deep male voice from nearby.

Betha pulled away when she realized that a few Others had joined them—shifters, by their eye colors. The brightest greens, blues, and golds usually were the tell.

Angie smiled at Betha and motioned toward the two guys. "Oh, Betha, this is Ben and Joey. They are Pack. Ben is the one with the dark hair—he's a teddy bear. Joey is so not a teddy bear, but everyone loves him anyway."

Betha sized up the two guys carefully. Ben was broad, built like a football player, with a kindness in his gaze that spoke of some amount of wisdom despite his youth. Joey, though, looked like a blond surfer. His rambunctious grin was contagious, and Betha smiled in response. Both of the shifters blushed slightly at the attention and waved awkwardly in response to Angie's teasing introduction, as though they were shy or not used to meeting other people.

Joey's nose wrinkled a little as he got closer, and he looked like he was going to sneeze. "What are you?" sputtered out of his mouth, his bright blue eyes focused on Betha.

Angie glared at him, her eyes wide. At the same time, Ben elbowed him in the side, none too gently.

Betha turned bright red before replying. "Human all the way. Sorry, not sorry." She gave a little self-conscious shrug.

Ben flashed her a bright white smile and held out his

hand. “It’s nice to meet you, Betha. Ignore the puppy here. Totally smooth. We are heading to the Pack lunch.” Betha shook his hand slowly, wondering what he was talking about. What lunch?

Angie’s eye bugged a bit, stepping away from Betha’s side. “Shoot, I can’t be late again. I’ll catch up with you this evening?” she said to Betha. The conflict was clear on Angie’s face as she looked at Betha’s bags.

Betha quickly spoke up. “It's all okay. Maybe we are in the same dorm?”

An unfamiliar female voice caused everyone to turn. “Angie is in the Pack dorms, but I can help you with your stuff. I’m one of the student check-in coordinators for new transfer students.”

Angie smiled at the newcomer, then gave Betha a nod. “Text me your room number when you get a chance. I’ll come visit and help you settle in.” With that, the three shifters quickly headed down the street toward one of the bigger buildings, walking in a tight triangle, the two boys leading with Angie in the rear. Angie glanced back once, but Betha sent her a thumbs-up.

“I need your name so I can look up what room you’re in. My name is Susan, by the way.” The woman’s voice was sweet as cherry pie, which made Betha smile. She felt a bit more comfortable now that she had seen Angie, and this woman was definitely putting her at ease.

“It is Betha, Betha Dubios.”

“It’s nice to meet you, Betha. Let me pull up your info.” Susan typed in a few letters on the tablet she pulled out. “Found you. You are in dorm C, bottom floor, number fourteen. It’s one of the quieter dorms. Looks like you are studying business? Me too. We might have some classes together." Susan smiled reassuringly. She glanced at the duffle bag, then at Betha, sizing her up. "I can grab the duffle, 'cause I think it's the size of you."

Betha couldn't help but giggle. "I mean, I am short, but I don't know if I would fit." Betha blushed as she studied the bag. "Nope, I totally think I could fit in it." Both of them laughed as Susan grabbed the bag and started down the walkway. Betha had learned to laugh at how short she was, but at least Susan didn't tower over her. The woman only had a few inches on her.

"So, how do you know Angie? I mean, she's, like, a Pack princess," asked Susan.

"Oh, we went to middle school together and stayed in touch after she changed. Angie still came home for the summers, and we would hang out. What's a Pack princess?" Betha knew their relationship was weird. Most humans didn't hang out with Others. At least it was that way in her small town. Which meant her being at this school was weird too. Or maybe not.

Susan nodded as they passed other students walking by. "I meant nothing negative by it. It's just, the rumor is she is the last one of her kind. Or at least that's what people said a few years ago. Yet she is nice as heck, which makes it hard to be jealous." Everyone seemed to smile at the two of them, and Betha hoped everyone would be as friendly as they seemed. The trees provided some shade from the sun, but it was still warm. The path wound closer to the brick buildings as they crossed the courtyard.

Betha struggled with the fast pace that Susan set.

"Yeah, she is always really sweet to me. My mom used to joke that we were sisters because of how we acted." Betha's head tilted to one side. "I'm glad that we finally get to hang out more now that we are both going to the same school." Betha had fallen behind by a step, which was why she noticed that Susan almost stumbled. Her blond hair went all over the place.

Susan quickly righted herself, but her voice seemed off as she spoke. "I hope so, since it seems like you guys are close. Just a heads-up, though—the various majors do tend to stick together. Same with the different races. It can be a bit cliquish here. There aren't many humans since the school is on Pack lands. Angie might have vouched for you, which should keep you in good shape with the Pack, but..." Susan shrugged before grabbing the door to enter the building. "You are just down the hall, lucky with a single." She opened the door with the number fourteen on it and quickly added, "Let me toss this on your bed, then I will grab your RA so you can get your keys."

Susan seemed to flee once Betha was in her room. Her manner had definitely changed when it became clear how close Betha was to Angie. The turn in conversation seemed to have spooked the girl. Betha turned toward the room and tried to not let Susan's comments get to her. The room was a good size, but it wouldn't take long for her to unpack. Her duffel was big, but it was all she owned in the world. She closed her eyes taking a deep breath.

I got this. It doesn't matter that I'm human. I can do this. In and out, just breathe in and out.

A knock on the open door caused her eyes to snap open. Susan was back with an elvish woman. Her tall ears poked out of her brown hair, sporting several piercings. "Hi, I'm Rielly, and I'm the Resident Assistant for this area." She held out her hand, and Betha shook it.

"It's nice to meet you..." Betha's voice trailed off as Rielly held on to her hand just a bit too long. The woman was looking at the birthmark on Betha's wrist.

"That is one weird tattoo," Rielly commented.

Betha pulled her hand back and shrugged. "It's a birthmark. I like to think it looks like a star."

Susan pinched her lips together like she wanted to say something but resisted.

Rielly shrugged and continued. "That's cool. Anyway, you can come to me with questions or problems. If anyone gives you shit about being human, text me—I'll deal with the assholes. Here is my number. Since this is older housing, I have the two lower floors. It is a quiet building. But yeah, if you need help, reach out. Otherwise, I have a few more check-ins to do." Rielly smiled at Susan. "Thanks for grabbing me. Today has been crazy."

Betha smiled as Rielly headed out, but Susan paused near the door, turning back toward her. "You should get that checked out. It looks like a sunspot to me."

Betha tilted her head in confusion. "You mean my birthmark? I have always had it. It's never caused me any problems."

Susan pointed to a spot covered up by her shirt. "I had one removed last year since the doctor was concerned. Figured I would mention it, just in case, plus the health center is free." Then Susan headed out, waving as she nearly fled again.

Once she was alone, Betha closed the door and rubbed her fingers over the mark on her wrist. Hopefully it wasn't a sunspot. The health center might be free, but she doubted it covered something like cancer. Medical bills were the last thing she wanted to deal with. Not again. Heck, she had just sold the house to pay off her mom's bills and cover her tuition here at St. Luna's.

Thinking of the house brought tears to her eyes. Crying would not help her unpack her things, or help get her a business degree, so she brushed them away. "You got this, Betha," she told herself. "Fake it 'till you make it."

CHAPTER TWO

Once they were out of Betha's hearing range, past the edge of the brick building, Angie reached out and punched Joey's arm hard. "What was with the 'What are you' bullshit? I warned you she was human. It's a sensitive subject, and you had to bring it up." Angie clenched her teeth and tried to calm down. She felt very protective of her friend.

Joey flinched, but for once he held his ground and didn't cower from Angie. "She isn't human! I don't know if you have really smelled her, but that's not a human scent." His eyes flashed to Ben, who nodded in agreement.

Ben added, "Joey's right, for once." He smirked at Joey, who nodded slightly, happy for the support even if it came with the jab. Ben continued, "You might be used to her scent, Angie, and just never noticed, but she's not human. No idea what she is. I haven't scented someone like that before, but yeah, not human. Though Joey is still a dick for bringing it up."

Angie released her jaw as she slowed down. She tried to concentrate on what Betha smelled like. Normally, she had the best nose out of the group. What Ben had said was true—she was used to her friend's scent. Betha was her oldest friend, and she had known her before her first shift. Maybe Angie hadn't noticed since Betha smelled like Betha had always smelled. Just like her mom. It didn't make sense, though. If Betha wasn't human, how had she gotten to her early twenties without discovering it? That just didn't happen anymore.

Her best friend did not manifest during their teens like most Others who weren't born to their truth, and Betha's mother, Josephine, had said that her family had always been human. It was one reason their parents had gotten along so well. Until Angie had manifested. Then Angie was the odd one out, though Betha and Josephine had always treated her the same. Then again, they did live in a very human-centric town where the only Other around was the monitor in the school. Had she really not ever noticed that her friend wasn't human? And if so, what was she?

The meeting bell rang, shaking Angie out of her thoughts, and they sped up toward Pack Hall. The large bell topped a steeple on Pack Hall, and it had gotten her into more trouble than anything else on campus. You could hear it from anywhere, and then you knew you were late to Pack Hall for something important. It rang only for Pack meetings and emergencies. The double doors were open, and she could see various Pack members gathered inside.

Angie realized the guys were waiting for an answer.

"I don't know. She didn't manifest. Her family has always been human, or so they said..." she trailed off, trying to make sense of it, but moving quickly to get into the hall without being too late.

Pack lunch was a weekly occurrence, but this was a special session for the start of the new school year. There were good things about having a college on Pack lands, but all the additional structure made Angie want to scream. It was hard enough having no choice for her junior high or high schools, having been forced to attend schools for newly manifested Pack members. Add in being away from Betha, her best friend, and it had been really rough. Now college, which was supposed to be a time to explore who she was and figure out what she wanted, had been taken away from her as well. The Pack was everywhere, and it encroached on her freedom constantly. It was only luck that Betha had gotten into St. Luna's. Well, that, or the threats Angie had made had actually been listened to.

Everyone had funneled down the entryway into the large open meeting room that made up most of the hall. It had giant glass windows on each wall and long tables set up for food. The windows always made her want to smile. Each pane had a different shifter in stained glass. The wolves were represented, along with the cats, the bears, and many others. Near the front of the hall, a giant black wolf was shown sleeping. It represented her kind, the Shadow Wolves, which had been thought nearly extinct. At the front of the hall, a small, raised stage with a podium took up the center. Angie took a seat in the back, along with Joey and Ben, who were staying quiet on the subject of Betha's humanness now that they saw how riled up Angie was. They all sat down just as Justin, the Pack leader, took the stage. It had been close, but they were not late. Not this time, anyway.

Angie couldn't help her thoughts wandering back to Betha and why she didn't show any signs of being Other. Ben's elbow hit her side, and her attention snapped to the front. Justin was talking about new training schedules and something about a potential curfew. It seemed like the same old Pack nonsense, and none of it was important to her. Most of the Pack bullshit didn't seem important to her, which was probably the main reason she kept getting into trouble. She really didn't understand why she had to follow all of these Pack rules all of the time.

Justin's voice rang out, drawing her attention. "You need to keep alert, and security is going to be increasing on campus. I will assign everyone shifts along with additional training sessions on the calendar. They will be based on your school schedule if you are actively taking classes. Be on the alert for anything out of the normal. If you smell sulfur, or if you feel static in your fur, report it in immediately."

Angie had more important things on her mind, like Betha and why, or how, she had gotten to this point without knowing what she was. The more she thought about it, the more she doubted that Betha was human, though she still couldn't explain why she hadn't noticed before. Betha was her chosen family, though she wasn't always sure that Betha understood what that meant. Maybe if her friend realized she wasn't human and figured out what she was, Betha would realize how amazing she was. Maybe, just maybe, Angie could help her crawl out of her shell.

Ben passed her a dish of mashed potatoes now that Justin had left the stage, and Angie's mouth watered, her mind shifting gears. The butter was melting on top, and she could smell the heavy cream that it was laced with. "Maybe I can have Justin take a sniff at her and see what he thinks," Angie mumbled under her breath. Her gaze traveled down the table, looking to see what was else on the menu. Multiple slabs of roast beef were spread out, with vegetables, gravy, and thick, fresh bread.

Ben looked at Angie in confusion. "What are you talking about? You better check your schedule. Justin mentioned changes while you were chasing butterflies in your brain. Don't pull a Joey." His head tilted toward Joey, who was scarfing down food, seemingly not paying attention to anything. He had gotten mashed potatoes on the table near his elbow.

Angie couldn't help but smile. Joey was adorable in his own way, and if things were different, she would totally date him. She had a Joey-sized soft spot that she tried to keep hidden. "Be nice, Ben. He can't help being, well, Joey."

"Yeah, you should be more like me," said Joey as he grabbed another fluffy roll to add to his plate. He flashed Ben his puppy dog look, making his eyes look huge.

Ben's eyebrows drew together. "Joey, you know better than to play that card with me. You play up what they expect of you, hitting on all the girls and dodging out of work." He turned back toward her. "Angie, you need to get your head in the game. Look around—that was a serious conversation. Something is going on. Not to mention you know the council is watching you." He gave her a pointed look, and Joey's carefree attitude vanished.

At the mention of the council, Angie rolled her eyes. It was a touchy subject, and one she did not want brought up during lunch. Betha was her primary concern. She didn't need to be thinking about how she only had two more years of relative freedom. Then she would be drafted, and things would get seriously less fun.

"There's nothing to worry about. They are probably just trying to spice up the new school year. You know Justin likes the Pack to be overprepared and hypervigilant." The sass could be heard in her voice. Angie had spent a good chunk of her time being made to overprepare and train with Justin.

Ben shook his head. "I don't know, Angie, it didn't sound like that. You really should have paid attention." He chewed on his lip as he loaded his own plate of food.

"It'll be fine. Just watch. This is going to be an amazing school year." As her mind wandered back to her friend and how glad she was that Betha had made it here, she knew she was right. This would be a great year, no matter what. She was going to make damn sure of it.

CHAPTER THREE

"Freak! Animal lover! Devil's Mark!"

Eight-year-old Betha rushed down the sidewalk, trying to get home without falling. Everything was so big and hazy. Giant kids made out of dark shapes chased her toward her house, calling names at her. Her shoe caught on a sidewalk crack, and she stumbled, catching herself on her hands. Sharp pain jolted up her arms as her palms hit the sidewalk.

"Loser!"

She got back to her feet as the ghostly children drew closer. The front door was open, and she rushed inside, sobbing. The lighting changed as she crashed to the floor. It was like the day changed from midafternoon to moonrise. The shadowy tormentors were gone, and this darkness felt safe. She sobbed quietly on the floor.

Footsteps sounded close by, and Betha flinched. She didn't know how much more of this she could take.

"Oh, Betha. Shhhh. I got you." Her mother pulled her into her arms in the foyer as she joined her child on the floor. Betha knew this couldn't be real, yet she wanted to stay in this moment forever.

"They were being mean, called me names, and made fun of my mark." Betha kept crying as she spoke, trying to get the words out. The part of her that was watching this flinched. She remembered the mean kids, especially after Angie left.

"It'll be okay, honey." Her mother flipped over Betha's wrist and kissed the mark. "I used to have a mark like yours, see?" She held up her own wrist where, if you looked super closely, there might be a little star. "You have nothing to worry about, not for a few years, anyway."

Betha snuggled into her mom's arms even more as she wiped away her tears. "I miss Angie and want to go to school with her."

"Honey, I know you miss your friend, but you can't go to school with Angie. That's not how the world works." She pulled her daughter tight, and Betha could smell the rose perfume her mom always wore. "When you are older, you will need to make choices, but for now, you get to be human. It's a blessing, dear. Be normal for as long as you can."

~

A RINGTONE SNAPPED Betha awake from her mother's arms, and it was all she could do not to groan. A floral scent seemed to linger around her, but it faded quickly. Her nails dug into her palms, helping her focus on something other than the emotional pain. Her mom, whole and talking to her, had been a gift, but it also hurt. A lot. And now, she needed to wake up.

Nightmare or dream, whatever you wanted to call it —that moment was precious, and Betha wanted it back. Her breath moved over her lips, and she focused on that instead of digging her nails in again. In, out, repeat. Just breathe. Finally, she opened her eyes to fumble in the light from her phone to see what time it was. The time showed a bright and early 6:00 a.m., along with several notifications and a few text messages.

"You didn't text me! You don't love me anymore ;P" read the most recent one.

Betha rolled her eyes at the text and sent over her room number. It was early, but her first class was early. The 6:00 a.m. wake up gave her an extra half hour before the alarm was supposed to go off. Time was precious, necessary to get ahold of her emotions, and maybe get some food.

Her phone went off again. "Be ready in 30. We can get breakfast together!"

She sent off a heart to Angie before turning her phone to vibrate. Betha grabbed her bathroom gear to get ready for the day, groaning inwardly but knowing it was important.

It didn't take her the whole half hour to get ready, and as she finished, she realized she was giddy to get breakfast with her bestie. That they could grab food together at any time was amazing, and it banished some of the lingering loneliness from the dream. There was a knock on her door, and she opened it to Angie. Her friend's long, dark hair was down and shiny. She was wearing only a little bit of makeup, yet she looked flawless, like she had since junior high.

"Morning! I know the best place to grab some bacon before classes start." Angie pulled Betha into a hug and only quickly glanced around the room before dragging Betha down the hall. "We need to hurry if we want to get in line before it gets crowded."

Betha scurried after her friend, wishing she had longer legs and sunglasses. The cooler morning was refreshing for August, even though the sun was already bright. "I bet it's going to be a hot one today."

"Probably. It gets muggier here than at home, I swear. Most of the buildings are air-conditioned though, so classes are usually okay."

It was hard to not stop and stare at the various buildings on campus, or the people walking by. She wasn't used to seeing elves, shifters, and trolls so casually. The elves seemed to stick together, but they all had long flowing hair that put even Angie's dark locks to shame. The shifters moved quicker than everyone else, and seemed to move with purpose, usually in small groups. The trolls still shocked her with their height, bright or dark green skin, and horns. So many different shapes of horns, some of them carved and decorated. She had to remind herself the rest of the world was like this, not as insanely human-centric as home. Well, her former home. *"This is home, now,"* thought Betha. But out loud, she asked, "So, how was the Pack lunch?"

Betha swore she could feel Angie roll her eyes. "It was the same old routine—stay safe, be careful of the new students on campus, earn good grades. All the stuff that we already know. Tension seemed high, but no one was actually talking about anything interesting." Angie grabbed Betha's hand and pulled her through a doorway, out of the sunlight. "We beat the rush. Breakfast sandwiches and coffee for the win!"

Angie's energy in the morning was always high, but this seemed to be a bit much even for her. Then they were surrounded by the smell of coffee, light guitar music, and the bustle of a café early in the morning. Betha recognized it as the coffee shop on campus she had once visited when applying to attend St. Luna's.

"This place looks awesome, just like I remember," said Betha as she glanced around.

Angie nodded, looking at the board. "It is the best place on Pack lands to get caffeine. I spend a lot of time here trying to get away from it all. You are going to want the bacon, egg, and cheese sandwich, with extra bacon—trust me, it's the best!"

Betha detected a note of something in Angie's voice. Angie had struggled to leave home in middle school to move here, but it sounded like it was more than that. "I thought you loved it here?"

Angie shook her head slightly, putting the conversation off as she moved in front of the register. "I'll order for us if you want to grab that free table by the window?" Angie turned to the barista at the counter.

The subject change was one that Betha was going to need to ask about at some point, but this was her first day. She didn't want to sour it this early if Angie didn't want to talk about it. Betha nodded and headed toward the table Angie had spotted. It was practically a rule whenever Betha went to a coffeeshop —always grab a table in a café, because they filled fast and stayed full. The warmth of the room eased some of the tension from her dream. She would be spending time here if she could. The smell of coffee was comforting, and it was from coffee she didn't even need to make. While she would miss her job as a barista, it was nice to be at a coffee shop that she wasn't working in.

It didn't take long for Angie to come over with two cups and a bag full of sandwiches. "I got you an iced mocha, along with a sandwich."

They both took a moment to take sips and start in on the food. The mocha was perfect. The right blend of chocolate and espresso, which wasn't bitter at all. At the same time, it wasn't too sweet. Angie had two sandwiches to work through, having always had a healthy appetite. To Betha's surprise, Angie continued the conversation.

"I like it here. There is just pressure to be perfect, since I am what I am. Never be the only one of your species, if possible." Angie stuck out her tongue.

"At least you have friends and family here to help you," replied Betha.

Angie turned a little sheepish. "I didn't mean to complain. The last few months for you must have sucked with your mom."

"I dreamed of her this morning. It was a dumb dream with bullies, but she was there from before and getting a hug was amazing. To be that young again..." Betha took a large sip of her mocha to make sure her eyes didn't tear up. The quick degradation her mother had gone through over the summer shocked even the doctors. It was still a raw subject for her.

Angie said, "Well, you have me now, all the time." She grabbed Betha's hand and gave her a soft smile. "Friends forever, no matter what. Don't forget it."

Betha gazed back at Angie and let a bit of a smile show on her face. "Thanks, I needed to hear that. It has been crazy."

"Did you get enough to share?"

Angie jerked back from Betha as Joey grabbed at the bag of sandwiches. "Ass, we were having a private conversation!" Angie said to Joey.

"The line is out the door and I got to get to class." Joey totally did the puppy dog look at the both of them. "I'll be your newest BFF, plus we all know that I am the hot one." He ran his fingers through his blond hair and batted his blue eyes at both of them, emphasizing his surfer-style good looks. Betha just shook her head in amazement, laughing at him. Joey continued, "See, I got you laughing. That needs to count for something."

Betha finished up her sandwich. "Well, I am not the one with the sandwiches, and I already have a BFF."

"Ah. But I can be your backup, ready to make you laugh. Or you can hit me repeatedly. Both work. Though since you gals don't have any sandwiches to spare, I am going to head to class. I don't want to be late on the first day." With that, Joey headed out, skirting the line that had formed out the door while the two had been talking.

"Is he always like that?" asked Betha.

"Yep. But he grows on you. Anyway, he is right. We should start heading that way as well. Friday we should go out and celebrate your first week on campus, along with the start of our junior year of college." Angie looked hopefully at Betha. "The guys might come, but that's just to keep us entertained," she added, hoping to get Betha to agree.

"I don't know..." Betha wasn't one to go out. The last two years had been about focusing on class, getting good grades, working to help pay the bills, and then taking care of her mother. She didn't have much practice with social settings.

"Pretty please? You know you want to. We can get all dressed up and just dance," begged Angie.

"Fine, but you're worse than Joey, and I have nothing to wear!" Betha said. She got up and grabbed her bag along with her mocha. It was to be savored during her first class of the day. Economics first thing in the morning was going to be rough.

"Ah, but I am prepared for that!" Angie's eyes glittered as she gathered up the garbage. "This is me. I know your size and I have just the thing!"

Grinning despite her nerves, Betha felt comforted. Maybe it was the coffee, but even heading to economics, it felt like it would all work out.

CHAPTER FOUR

Betha's first week of classes was finally done. Being mindful of money and her scholarship, she had packed in more than the required five courses. She was taking seven, with the goal of graduating a semester early. Thankfully, since it was the first week, most of her classes were only doing a general overview, laying out the timing of projects, and assigning what to read for next week.

Still, it had been exhausting. Her concerns about being one of the few human students had turned out to be justified. None of the teachers or students treated her differently, really, but it was still weird. Susan had asked her in economics if she had gotten the mark looked at yet. Betha sheepishly let her know that she hadn't. Talking with her, Betha realized she wasn't sure what Susan was. She seemed human, but her skin was almost perfect, more perfect than human skin had a right to be. It was almost like a vampire's skin, or one of the angelic bloodlines. It still wasn't clear to Betha if she could just ask or if that would be impolite.

Now that her first week was done and it was a glorious Friday, Betha decided to tackle it, face her anxiety, and just get the student health clinic visit over with. The waiting room smelled like herbs and sunshine, yet it didn't ease her tension. For a moment, the memory of hearing the doctor talking to her about her mother's diagnosis crashed on her. She had been in a similar room when she learned that her mother wasn't ever going to get better, and the emotional shock had taken her breath away momentarily.

"Betha Dubios?" said a strong male voice.

Her head snapped up, and she smiled at the doctor as she got to her feet, banishing the memory.

"Follow me," he said. Betha followed the doctor into one of the examination rooms. "Take a seat." Once she sat down, he closed the door and took the other seat. "So, what brings you in today? You mentioned you had a mark you wanted someone to look at."

"Yes." She turned her wrist up and pointed to the birthmark. "Someone mentioned it might be a sunspot, so I figured it would be good to get it checked out. I know cancer can be bad news."

The doctor took one glance at the mark and laughed, causing Betha to jump as her voice trailed off at the end of her explanation. "That's a good one. Who put you up to this?" He said, smiling at her. Then confusion slowly came over his face. "Wait, you are serious."

"As serious as I can be—what's wrong?" she asked, concerned, and starting to be a little annoyed.

The doctor grabbed a wet wipe and took her wrist. He wiped it over the mark and froze when it didn't vanish. "That's not possible." He pulled out her file, flipping through the pages, looking for something. "You are messing with me—you have to be. Did one of my colleagues put you up to this? I'm already embarrassed that Traveler Kyra wouldn't let me publish my thesis."

Betha shook her head, her stomach seemed to flip, and her chest ached. "What? I don't know what you are talking about!" she exclaimed, as he seemed to be talking to himself more than to her.

He studied her face, then went back to the files, his brown hair falling in his face. The glasses outed him as a human. "Your file lists you as human—which can't be correct. That's definitely a Traveler's mark, but Traveler Kyra said she was the only one on Terra..." The young doctor rambled on, completely ignoring Betha. He logged into the computer and searched for a few moments. His fingers clicked on the keyboard loudly. "You even have a small feeling of power emanating from you, which would be what I would expect, since you don't have any Anchors," he continued, still mostly ignoring Betha as she got more and more agitated.

Betha's breathing sped up, and the room wobbled a bit. "I think you are mistaken. I'm human. My whole family is human. And what do boats have to do with anything?" The dream flashed to the front of her mind, where her mom pointed out her own mark that had faded. Was that a memory? Her hands felt cold and clammy at the same time her forehead began to sweat.

Was she not human?

"See, it's the same mark!" The excited doctor brought up a drawing of a similar mark that was darker and had other designs outside of the star. "Traveler Kyra has multiple Anchors, signified by the extra marks around the star."

Betha didn't even blink while looking at the screen. It was hard to get air in her lungs.

The doctor's voice paused as he really looked at Betha. "I think you need some water. You are looking quite pale." He opened the door and leaned out into the hall, calling for a glass of water with some panic in his voice. It didn't take long for an elven healer to come in with some water and a concerned face.

"I gave her a bit of a shock, I'm afraid. She just found out she is a Traveler. Her file lists her as human. I thought she was pranking me because of the rejection of my thesis..." The doctor trailed off as the healer narrowed her pale eyes at him and motioned him out the door.

"How about I take it from here?" the elven woman said. He nodded his head thankfully before giving a sheepish smile at Betha and then fleeing the room.

"Try to take a deep breath, dear." The healer spoke softly and handed her the glass of water. "I am sorry for his manner. That doctor is better with research than with people. This seems to have come as a surprise to you. Did you not know?"

Betha shook her head as her eyes watered.

The healer continued, "Usually one of your parents is a Traveler, and you would know it by this point. They would have told you about your power. You look to be in your twenties, though, so you still have time to figure this out. It's not too late yet."

"I don't even know what a Traveler *is.* My mom mentioned having a mark at some point, but hers was faded," said Betha in a small voice, trying to make sense of the shock.

The healer nodded her head understandingly. "That means your mother made the choice to not have any Anchors. It could be why you are listed as human, though you should have gone to an Other school to prepare yourself for your own choice."

Again, Betha shook her head no, and a look of worry crossed the healer's face.

"This is definitely an unusual situation. I will send a message to your adviser, and we can get you into some beginner classes that we have for humans that manifest later in life—usually in their late teens. You might feel a little out of place, but trust me, it will help." A soft warmth seemed to come over Betha as the healer smiled and took her hand. "I will also send some resources for you to read over the weekend. You might hear from your adviser before Monday, but things are hectic around here at the moment. I don't doubt that once Traveler Kyra is alerted to you, she will take you under her wing." A troubled look flickered over the healer's face, then vanished.

The warmth continued to flow over Betha, and the tension that was in her chest lessened. Most of the panic seemed to have faded. The woman let go of her hand and patted Betha on the shoulder. "You might want to reach out to your mother's family as well to get their take on this."

Betha's words tumbled out of her mouth before she could filter them. "I can't. My mother is at Luna's Grace with early dementia. She was the only family I had."

The silence after she said "Luna's Grace" was so very loud. Luna's Grace was where folks went to die. The healer looked conflicted at the news, but solemnly nodded. "That would be the Traveler's curse, dear," the older woman said softly. The edges of the room dimmed a bit, and Betha felt more warmth from the healer's hand on her shoulder. "No fainting on me, dear. The paperwork is a hassle." She chuckled, probably trying to lighten the mood.

The warmth cleared up Betha's vision, and the glass of water was cool in her hand. She took several sips from it, trying to steady herself. It helped, and she let the information sink in.

"Her illness is a curse?"

"Yes, well, from what we know. Some call it a choice. She decided not to Anchor herself to enough people. You have an increased likelihood to have memory issues if you make that choice, but don't worry, you have plenty of time before you need to decide. You are in the best place to learn what you need to. Part of the school's mission is to help integrate manifested humans into the Other population." The healer motioned to the glass of water. "Drink up. While this might feel overwhelming, you are at the best place you can be for this sort of news."

Betha drank, but could only think, "*This may be the best place, but that doesn't make this any easier. What the hell am I?*"

CHAPTER FIVE

Being invited out was definitely a cool new thing for Betha, but walking around Pack housing had been an intense experience. It felt like eyes were watching every step she took. When she glanced around, she would catch shifters staring at her, every time. The feeling of not belonging was smothering, especially on top of feeling unsettled from the doctor's appointment, which she was absolutely trying to not think about. Paranoia was not a good look on her. Betha had to remind herself that she was invited to go over and get dressed with Angie. Not to mention, Angie had clothes for her to wear. Betha certainly didn't have anything appropriate for a night out in public.

Betha knocked on Angie's door, shifting her weight from foot to foot. Because she had never been to the Pack housing, she had given herself lots of time. To her surprise, Angie's room had been very easy to find, and now Betha hoped she wasn't too early. Another door down the hall opened, and Betha flinched. To her surprise, Ben stepped out of the room, pausing when he saw her standing awkwardly by Angie's door.

"Hey, Betha. Angie should be getting out of training shortly. Are you going dancing with us tonight?" asked Ben.

Betha smiled a little shyly. "Yeah, Angie invited me to go out and celebrate. I guess she even has a dress picked out for me."

"I can see her doing that. She would probably love to dress you up like a doll. Normally she is surrounded by guys in the Pack." Ben looked down the hall, and his smile grew bigger. "There she is. It was great seeing you again. I'm looking forward to tonight!" He gave her a wave and started down the hall away from her.

Betha looked over her shoulder, but she didn't see anyone. She knitted her brows, wondering what Ben had meant, but after a moment she heard someone coming up the stairs.

Angie smiled as she came out of the stairwell, meeting Betha's eyes. "I didn't expect you to arrive before me. I figured I would need to drag you out of your dorm room." Her eyes narrowed a bit. "Though you are looking a bit...stressed. Do I need to beat someone up?"

Betha moved to the side so Angie could get to her door. "No. It was just a long day. I'll catch you up while we get ready. Plus, I saw Ben and he is excited to go dancing—we can't disappoint him!" She couldn't help but wink at Angie, and she heard a male chuckle from down the hall.

Betha popped into Angie's room as her friend

motioned her forward. “Holy smokes, this is not dorm housing,” exclaimed Betha. The room had a seating area and two open doors. One led to a bedroom and the other to a private bathroom. “How do I get housing like this?” There was even a hardwood floor instead of the typical commercial laminate in Betha’s room.

“Well, this is Pack housing. It’s basically an apartment, but with just a mini fridge and a microwave for a kitchen. Most of us split our time between going to classes here and up in the mountains with the Pack. It’s nice, given the classes I’m taking, and as a shifter I like having people around me. Well, only certain people.”

Was that sadness I heard?

“Ben said you had training?” asked Betha, hoping Angie would fill her in on her day before Betha had to take her turn. Procrastination was key in the face of stress.

“Yeah, I will need to shower. I have training every Monday, Wednesday, and Friday afternoon. It’s part of my class schedule. Gotta stay in fighting shape, though lately, it has been a bit more intense than normal. Like, they added an additional thirty minutes a day.” Angie rolled her eyes, then shook her head and motioned toward the bathroom. “So, do you want to shower first, or should I?”

“I should be good.” Angie’s nose twitched. “Or not.” Betha awkwardly chuckled.

Angie grinned at her friend. “Sorry, I can tell you were sweating and worried about things. A shower will help with that. I didn’t want to bring it up if you didn’t want to talk about it.”

Betha moved toward the couch. “We can talk about it,” she said hesitantly. Despite her anxiety, Angie was her best friend, and it didn’t take long for Betha to catch her up on the doctor and healer visit.

Angie leaned back on the couch with awe on her face. “No wonder you need a shower. You have been thrown for a loop. Fuck, does this mean your mom knew and didn’t tell you? I can’t believe you are a Traveler. I have only heard some stories. Heck, most of them would qualify as legends.”

Betha held up her wrist as Angie’s eyes darted that way. “Yeah, this is the mark of a Traveler. I spent this afternoon reading a bit of the stuff the healer sent over. There wasn’t a ton of information. I am basically human unless I make the choice to Anchor my soul with someone. Which I don’t really understand. Oh, and I have a fifty-fifty shot of turning out like my mom if I opt out.” At the mention of her mom, tears began to well up in her eyes. Angie leaned in for a hug, which let the waterworks loose.

“How could she not tell me? She knew what was happening and didn’t even warn me. I have been watching as she just got worse and worse, and now she doesn’t even know me most of the time,” Betha said through her tears.

“Shh. It’s all right, get it all out.” Angie hugged Betha tightly and started to rub her back to calm her down, though Betha could tell she had soaked Angie’s shirt with her tears.

As Betha thought more about the situation and ran to the end of her tears, the grief began to be replaced with anger. "I had to sell the house, the only place I had ever lived. And now I am a Traveler. Turns out I have never been human. Or rather, I am human, unless I bond with someone. I literally have to bond my soul with someone, or I can lose myself to the universe. I have gone my whole life thinking I was human, and that was a lie. I would have given anything to be able to go with you after you changed."

Anige snorted. "Being an Other isn't the be-all and end-all. We are subject to the draft, unlike humans. You had no need to train for the possibility of serving in the Guard, since we protect humanity as part of the Accords. Not to mention, in the case of shifters, you have to listen to your Alpha. It isn't all roses. While you were wishing you could join me, there were times I wished I didn't manifest. Either way, it doesn't change the situation you find yourself in now. It will all be okay. I know you are frustrated at your mom, but at least you are in the right place to learn. Saint Luna's is literally set up for adult changes."

Betha stilled for a moment as Angie's words washed over her. She knew being an Other had its downsides. "She told me to go here. She made me promise to come here for school."

"Maybe she couldn't tell you and knew you would be okay if you went here. Plus, your mom always loved me. She knew I would have your back no matter what. And I didn't have a choice about coming here." Betha noticed that this was the second time Angie had brought up choices. It seemed they needed to have some more one-on-one time to discuss what was weighing on her.

"Travelers get Anchors and protect the portals which connect to the leylines," said Angie. "We learned about it in school. You will probably need to take some classes to catch up, but I can help."

Betha pulled back from Angie. "You mean we bond with Others, and steal their powers, and have to protect magical doorways? Yeah, something like that—"

Angie's voice rose in slight anger as she cut Betha off. "It doesn't work that way. It's a choice for both of them, and they share powers. It is a huge gift to be an Anchor. It's a great honor. Grandpappy is one."

Betha's eyes grew wide. "Grandpappy is an Anchor?" She blinked a few times. "How did I not know that?" They had spent time with Grandpappy when Angie was home for the summers. She was required to have a shifter nearby in case she lost control, and he would always join them on their trips so they could spend time together. Now that she thought about it, it might have been the only reason Angie was allowed to go home during the summers.

"He doesn't talk about it. I think he is much older than my great-grandfather. Like, a few more greats, since he bonded with his Traveler."

"That's amazing," Betha muttered. If Grandpappy was an Anchor, that meant he knew a Traveler. And if he knew a Traveler, maybe there was one that she might be able to talk to.

"How about I take the first shower? Then I will get ready when you shower, and that way I can help you with your makeup. We should call Grandpappy—I bet he can come to visit. Here, I'll call him and see what he suggests."

Angie quickly dialed a number on her phone before Betha could stop her. "Hey Grandpappy—I am not in trouble! You remember Betha? Well, it turns out she is a Traveler...Wait, you knew? No, she didn't know. It was a shock. Yeah, she has a ton of questions...That would be amazing! Love you tool. Bye-bye."

Betha wiggled her eyebrows. "So?"

"He is coming for a visit, and he is going to reach out to his Traveler. He thought you knew, or he would have said something before. Now, I am going to take that shower."

The fact that someone who actually knew what all of this meant was on the way came as a huge relief to Betha. Maybe once Grandpappy showed up, she would have some answers and things would start to make sense again. It was enough of a relief that she could put it all out of her mind and focus on going out tonight. Maybe she could even enjoy herself, though at some point she would need to circle back to the tension that Angie was showing. Maybe Angie wasn't as happy as Betha thought she was.

~

Angie let the hot water wash over her. Betha was an actual Traveler—it was almost unbelievable. If Betha wanted to bond with her, it would change everything. It seemed like a mirage or a miracle. Yet, Angie didn't want to pressure her into anything. They mostly didn't keep secrets from one another, but there were a few things that Angie had kept to herself. Maybe now it was time to talk to Betha about them. She would understand. And maybe they could help free each other from their respective fates.

CHAPTER SIX

Betha's thighs kept sticking together in the heat, and while she could handle heels for a length of time, waiting in line was getting to be a bit much, and her feet were starting to hurt. At least they were moving every couple of minutes. It seemed they were letting people in after checking IDs, so at least they weren't going to be stuck out in the muggy air forever. She had to give it to Angi—the short, blue dress did look amazing with her hazel eyes. It showed a lot of thigh, but that didn't bother her. The guys in line seemed to be appropriately impressed, and that helped her forget everything else from earlier in the day. Angie had blow-dried her hair after she had gotten out of the shower, and it was now curled about her face. She should have guessed that Angie was so good at hair and makeup, given how amazing she looked every day.

"They have the best drinks here, plus it tends to not be as loud since shifters love the place," Angie commented, filling the silence while they waited.

Betha nodded, wondering how much longer this was going to take. Having her feet hurt all night was not the plan. Her eyes caught on a sign that was taped near the door as they moved closer.

"Ugh, Angie," she motioned toward the sign, "No humans allowed?"

"That's new, like brand new. Something was mentioned for humans at the Pack lunch today—I didn't think much of it." Angie shrugged before pulling out her phone.

"Will I be able to get in?" asked Betha.

"Didn't we just spend this afternoon on this topic? Silly Betha." The group in front of them was let into the club, and now it was their turn.

The bouncer looked them over and shook his head. "No humans tonight. They have a curfew."

Angie grabbed Betha's wrist and turned it over. "Traveler—not human." He took a sniff at Betha, and confusion showed on his face. He shook his head doubtfully, clearly not sure what to make of Betha. "Only if you are vouching, princess."

"Of course I'll vouch for her," snapped Angie. "She's accompanying me, isn't she?"

The bouncer motioned toward the door, letting them go in. Betha tried to not look uncertain as they walked inside. "Thanks, Angie. I don't think I could have done that."

"You are what you are. The sooner you accept that, the better. Plus, it got you in, didn't it?" Angie replied. Angie kept a hold of Betha's hand as she started to weave through the crowd. "Oh! The guys got a booth. Wicked!"

Angie said under her breath as she got a message on her phone.

The music wasn't too loud, which surprised Betha, and it wasn't too crowded either. Neon dance music kept her head bopping to the beat. Bright lights flashed randomly from under the dance floor as they weaved across, doing their best to get to the booth the guys had grabbed while keeping away from the couples dancing. The overall vibe was lights flashing, music playing, and people having fun with lots of nice shirts and slacks on the guys, and short dresses with low necklines on the girls. Then Betha was sliding into a corner booth with Angie on one side and Ben on the other. The booths were dimmer than the floor, but pendant lights hung over each table, providing a steady light instead of the flashing over the dancers.

Joey was near the edge of the booth, checking out the group of people dancing. "Now that everyone is here, I can grab the first round." He darted out into the crowd toward the bar as soon as Betha and Angie got seated.

"Do I smell or something?" asked Betha, trying to make a joke based on Joey's move-in day comments about her smell. "He took off pretty fast!"

Ben spoke up first. "He's just hoping to find someone special for the evening. I told him it would be rude to leave before you two got here, and he took that to the letter." Ben wiggled his eyebrows, and Betha couldn't help but laugh. His voice was so deep, but still easy to hear over the music. "What about you—looking for someone special tonight, Betha?"

Betha blushed as she answered, "Nah, tonight is

about dancing and getting to know new friends like you and Joey." She was thankful that the dress wasn't cut low in the front, given how she was leaning over the table.

Angie elbowed her slightly, causing her to smile. "See," Angie interrupted, "I told you that you would get along with them." Betha wondered if this was what the year was going to be like. Taking classes, going out with her friends, and trying to figure out what being a Traveler even meant. If so, it would be an adventure, a fun one with friends. It could almost be normal.

"Drinks!" Joey announced as he returned, rather carefully setting down a bunch of drinks on the table. They all looked electric blue in the dim lighting. "Cheers! To our new friend, Betha!" He held his glass up and everyone quickly grabbed one and followed suit, chiming in with their own "Cheers!"

Betha took a tiny sip of the drink, wondering what it was. Angie leaned over, seeing the confusion on her face. "It's a blue light. Not too strong, but tasty. Doesn't leave a hangover unless you drink way more than you should."

Another sip proved that it was tasty, sweet, but not too sweet, and it didn't burn. It didn't take long before Betha could swear she was hearing a buzzing sound. The drink was smooth and slightly chilly, which helped with the heat. She had forgotten that Shifters gave off so much heat. When it had just been the two of them as teenagers, camping in the back yard, the heat coming off of Angie had been amazing. Now, being sandwiched between two of them in a booth was a bit much.

Betha realized that Joey was looking back and forth between her and Ben, not too subtly, along with giving glances at Angie. "You can use words," commented Betha. "At least, Angie assures me you can use words. What's on your mind?"

It was like her permission opened a fire hose, and Joey began to ramble, "So are you one of us? I have been trying to figure it out since we met you. Definitely not human, but something. My nose twitches when you are near. But you don't smell like one of us, either, not really. Not a shifter. Or an elf. I've got a couple of those in one of my classes."

Betha's mouth fell open, and her eyes opened wide before she turned toward Ben. "I thought you said I didn't smell!"

He flashed his sparkling whites at her, along with a smirk, but he just took a sip of his drink without answering. He leaned backward in the booth, a dark presence grinning at her with a glass of blue liquid.

Betha took another swig of the blue drink and turned back to Joey. "I just found out that I am a Traveler, like, this afternoon."

Joey reached out to grab Betha's wrist, but Angie smacked his hand before he could touch her. "You need to ask Betha first. That's not cool! You know better. Consent is a thing."

Joey's face fell, and he looked like a kicked puppy. "Sorry, Betha, can I see your mark?" he asked sheepishly.

Betha had the feeling that Joey didn't really think before he did things, and she wondered if that was always true. He seemed sweet, and totally had the puppy dog eyes down. At the same time, she already understood he used it to his advantage. Betha held out her wrist over the table so the mark was visible.

Joey's blue eyes grew wide. "That is so freaking cool! I thought Travelers were only, like, legends!"

"Nope, I'm definitely here in the flesh and blood," responded Betha. The dance music started moving faster and her fingers tapped on the table. "This is the second time you mentioned that I smell. I feel weird asking, but what do I smell like?"

To her surprise, it was Angie who spoke up first. "Summer twilight and family, but I thought that was normal. I didn't realize that you weren't human. Believe me, I would have told you." Betha believed that. The two of them had always hoped that Betha would end up being Other.

"Huh, my nose picks up a bit of dusk. What about you, brother bear?" asked Joey.

Ben rolled his eyes before replying, "I can smell the twilight and something else, but I can't put my finger on it. I can smell better in my other form. It's harder for me as a human."

"Well at least I don't smell bad." Everyone laughed at that one, and Betha couldn't keep the smile off her face. "Right?"

Angie couldn't help but add, "It isn't a smell, more like a scent."

Betha nodded her head like she understood the difference. She could get used to this. Hanging out with friends, not worried about money or taking care of her mother. School so far was amazing, and she felt like she might be the freest she had ever been in her life. Ben gave her another smile, and she started to work up the courage to ask him to dance. Going out dancing was a new thing for her, so she might as well get the party started. He was taller than her, and broad. But she somehow sensed he was also capable of being very gentle and careful with that large body of his. It would be fun to dance with him.

Then the buzzing sound she'd heard earlier increased, and she tilted her head slightly trying to figure out where it was coming from. It took her a moment to realize it wasn't in time with the music. Betha glanced around, trying to pinpoint it.

"Do you guys hear that? It's like static...or a buzzing sound?" asked Betha.

Ben and Joey shook their heads. Angie closed her eyes in focus for a moment before answering. "No buzzing or static. The music has been turned up a bit."

Betha shook her head. "It must be the blue light. Maybe it and Travelers don't mix." Her statement didn't stop her from going to take another sip. Pain lanced up her arm and the glass slipped through her fingers. "Ugh!"

Angie moved faster than possible and caught it, only spilling a bit of blue liquid on the table. "Whoa Betha, you okay?"

"That hurt, my mark just..." her voice trailed off as she realized everyone at the table wasn't listening. They were all looking toward the door. The music was suddenly cut, and she could finally hear the screams from outside. Screams of terror.

CHAPTER SEVEN

As Betha's mouth opened to ask what to do, Angie darted out of the booth using the same explosive speed that had let her catch the glass. Angie's eyes stayed on the door as she yanked her dress over her head. "Betha, you need to stay here—Joey," her eyes flicked over to him, "will stay with you. Ben and I need to move. Now!" Her mouth snapped shut, Angie was naked.

Joey moved to let Ben out of the booth, then perched on the edge of the seat, waiting for more instruction.

Others in the club burst into motion all at once. Some shifters stripped out of clothing before changing. Others didn't care, shredding clothing as people became wolves, bears and cats. The bartenders all grabbed weapons from somewhere out of sight. Betha realized that those must be guns. She'd seen them in movies and on TV, of course, but never in person. It was like everyone knew what to do without talking about it, and it was terrifying. The feeling of being very unprepared washed over her. The sign about humans being under curfew came to mind, and the fact that she probably should be back at the dorms right now. She may not be human, but that was a trivial detail; all Others were required to have basic defense training since they could be drafted in times of need. Some like shifters clearly went above and beyond that. It was obvious that they all knew what to do and she didn't.

"What's going on?" asked Betha, rubbing her wrist. Her mark was throbbing, and it felt like her wrist was being pulled toward something outside. Ben kicked off his shoes.

"Doesn't matter, you aren't prepared for it," Angie replied. Betha flinched at the raw honesty. She wasn't trained for this, and Angie knew that. And whatever this was, clearly it was dangerous. Angie tossed the dress and shoes into the booth.

"But..." Betha didn't have anything she could say, but she didn't want to be useless. The feeling of being a trapped animal while her friends went off to battle was palpable in her, but she had nothing to offer.

Angie and Ben darted toward the door and were gone in a heartbeat. They weren't the only ones who headed out the door, and the sudden departure of all of the people caused Betha to shiver. The screams outside got louder, and Joey grabbed her hand, yanking her under the table. It felt like she lost skin off the back of her thighs to the leather, he pulled her so hard.

"We are going to stay here and be very quiet, okay? Whatever is out there is bad. Angie and Ben got this; this is what they do," said Joey. His fingers tightened on her hand while his eyes strayed toward the door. He angled his body in front of her.

"Why can't we help?" asked Betha.

"Betha, I am a literal golden lab. The lowest on the shifter pole. I can basically bark at things, and I play a mean game of catch. You have no training. We need to stay out of the way and let the professionals handle this. If we get in the way, they have to protect us too, and that could get them killed."

The floor was sticky with spilled drinks and sweat, and she couldn't see much between the dim lighting and the cover of the table. The yelling grew louder. Joey froze, sensing something Betha couldn't, and slid a hand over her mouth. "Hush," he mouthed silently.

Something crashed through the door into the club, and more screaming started. It took so much to not whimper. Sweat dripped down her back, and her hands trembled as she tried to hold perfectly still. Her eyes focused on the green dress Angie had left on the seat that was next to her head.

Gunshots were fired, and something dark crashed onto the dance floor in front of the table. It was covered in fur and blood, but Betha had no idea what it could possibly be. Something animal-like, and she wasn't sure if it was a friend or foe. All she could do was pray to the fates that it wasn't one of her friends. It looked a little like a dog, but the head was too big, and it was ugly in a way no dog or wolf had ever been to Betha.

She opened her mouth to ask, but Joey shook his head, his eyes wide, looking beyond the body. All Betha could stare at was the blood pooling on the floor. It looked black in the dim light from the club.

Someone screamed again, in pain, but it was cut off. Joey started to shake, and Betha realized that it wasn't a good thing. The sound of silence in the nightclub was horrible, but Joey didn't move his hand. Betha pulled forward, but he shook his head hard again, motioning for her to be still.

Suddenly, something moved, and the table was ripped away as though it were made of paper by a massive paw. The pedestal that held the table hit Betha hard as it flipped away, knocking her forward. Joey's arm was yanked off her shoulder as something large grabbed at him.

"Betha, run!" he yelled.

He punched at a second fur-covered creature, its maw covered in red, dripping saliva. It must have come up from behind as their attention had been focused on the first one. Betha froze, huddled near the booth, staring in horror. Joey struggled with the dog-like animal. Its head was twice the normal size of a dog, and it had spikes and long claws. Like the first, it looked *wrong*, and ugly, in a way that Betha knew would haunt her nightmares. The creature ignored Joey's punches and stabbed forward with a massive paw, striking Joey's middle with wicked claws. It yanked Joey closer to its gaping maw. Then Betha heard screaming and realized a second later that *she* was screaming, and the dog-like horror looked at her. Large, red eyes glowed like hot coals as they stared at her. Its teeth were so big. It seemed to forget Joey, dropping him as it headed her way.

Darkness hit the side of the creature, plowing it away from them. Betha rushed forward and tried to stop the bleeding from Joey's wound with her hands. Joey's shirt was covered in blood, and she was pretty sure his stomach wasn't supposed to look like that.

"Please, run," he whispered weakly, looking at her.

The sound of something sniffing came near, and Beth looked up, smacking into a snout covered in blood. She flinched before she recognized the giant black wolf. Angie's wolf form was bigger than she remembered. She was so tall that she could look Betha in the eye as she sat on the floor, trying to help Joey. Angie whined as she sniffed at Joey, but he just looked relieved. Betha saw the creature on the ground behind Angie, its throat torn out and clearly not moving. Looking around, she saw the other creature on the dance floor was also down, surrounded by weapon-toting club staff.

Everything seemed to un-pause. People returned to the nightclub, and Betha could hear sirens in the distance. Her hand wrapped around Joey's, and she squeezed. "It is going to be all right. We will be okay," whispered Betha.

"We will," Ben echoed as he walked toward them. His clothing was gone, and Betha looked away, not wanting to see his naked body. "That's just a flesh wound, Joey will be fine."

Angie sat down on the floor next to Betha, breathing directly on her face. Her wolf breath was rough, but it was comforting having her friend near.

"What were those...things?" Betha motioned to the dead creatures on the floor after leaning away from

Angie a bit. The smell was horrible, like burnt rotten meat mixed with the copper of blood.

"A demon of some kind," answered Ben. "Probably what Justin was trying to warn us about in the Pack meeting." Betha saw a look pass between Ben and Angie, andAngie suddenly looked away. Betha's eyes grew wide, but she had no idea what to say. She didn't even know that demons were real.

Uniformed officials entered the room and started helping people up. Things were a bit hazy, and Betha couldn't really focus on anything. The commingled smells of blood and the dead demons were getting to her. "The buzzing is gone," she mumbled.

Angie froze and growled as someone approached.

"Medic and Guard. Please stand down," said a male voice that Betha didn't recognize. The growling stopped, but Angie stood up to sniff at them. The Guard was the Others' police and peacekeeping force, not a group to be taken lightly. Betha had seen them on the news growing up. The Guard handled the more major combat situations that came up when so many different types of people mixed. Scuffles, fights for leadership and such. Yet, she hadn't seen one in real life with black armor on. He literally had a sword on one side. Blood was splattered on his boots.

"We need to check out your friend." An elven healer stepped around the Guard, kneeling near Joey, and Betha could feel the warmth come off of her. "We are only closing it up so he can shift. He'll heal the rest on his own," the elven woman said.

The Guard looked at Ben, then at Betha. He had to be

an Other of some kind, but Betha didn't know what. He looked like a model—perfect skin that was nearly too white, and perfect physique, with an intense stare, all of which usually indicated a vampire. "I need statements from both of you. Miss, you said something about a buzzing?"

Betha kept her hand in Joey's as she looked up at the Guard. He must have realized how intimidating he was, since he crouched down pulling out a notebook. "We were drinking blue lights, and I started to hear static. It stopped after my mark flared," Betha said, trying to be helpful, though she didn't know what any of it meant.

Ben said, "She is a brand-new Traveler, Sir."

The Guard did a double take. "That would be why you didn't sound the alarm about the portal, as a Traveler should have."

Betha shook her head in confusion. "Alarm about a portal? What portal?"

"From the demon world." He stood back up and looked at Ben. "And you two? What's your story?" He motioned at Angie, who was still in shadow wolf form.

"We exited the building and began to fight back when we heard the screams. Thankfully, the Guard showed up," replied Ben. The Guard took more notes in his book. "What happened, Sir?"

"We were lucky is what happened—the portal was closed by Terra's Traveler who happened to be visiting. The fates were watching out for us tonight. Curfew is in effect; you all better get back to campus."

Betha realized that the Healer was done and had moved on. "But what about Joey?" He still seemed very weak and not at all okay, though he had stopped bleeding.

Ben moved toward his friend, kneeling. "I'll carry him to campus. We need to get back before they do a lockdown. Joey, you need to shift to fix this. You know better." Betha let go of Joey's hand and looked away, ignoring the sounds of bone crunching. When she looked back, Ben was picking up a golden lab in torn clothes. It looked like Joey was out cold. The shift must have taken everything he had left. Getting to her feet required Betha to breathe deeply several times, and even so she felt unsteady.

Betha did her best to stay on her feet and followed Ben, with Angie still in shadow wolf form beside her as they left the club. Angie's ears came up past her belly button. Outside, things were much worse. Blood was everywhere, and Guards were dodging around, helping people as best they could. Betha felt sick to her stomach seeing all of the carnage. She noticed several Guards freeze at the sight of Angie, then once they realized she was with them, relax.

I could have sounded an alarm? Could I have stopped this? Betha thought, hoping next time she would be more useful, and not knowing how.

CHAPTER EIGHT

Joey almost died tonight. I almost died tonight.

Betha's eyes stayed pinned to the ceiling from her spot on the bed. Joey, still in lab form, lay near her, and Ben had crashed on the other side of Joey. The four of them walked back to Angie's room because no one had wanted to be alone. Angie was in the shower, but Joey was still in dog form, sleeping on the bed. Hopefully, he was healing too. Ben was already sleeping on the other side of the bed. He had tried to get Betha's mind off of this evening by asking about her classes, but she couldn't keep the conversation going. Her blue dress from the club was in a trash bag, along with the shoes. Angie had taken one sniff of them and tossed them without missing a beat. Betha realized she hadn't grabbed Angie's clothes from the club, but her friend didn't seem to care.

It seemed that this was not the first time Joey and Ben had stayed over in Angie's room. It felt like a family who was trying to support one another, though Betha kept missing the steps, not knowing the cues. Right after the attack, coming back here had made sense, but now that her mind was racing, Betha couldn't believe she was in an oversized shirt and going to have a sleepover, with boys no less.

Whining came from the dog beside her, and she couldn't help but begin to pet Joey's back. "Shh. Joey, it's all okay now." Her voice seemed to calm him down, but she couldn't help the flashback to that thing's claws in his stomach. He'd told her to run, but she had frozen to the spot.

Next time...goddess, I hope there isn't a next time.

All of that blood in the parking lot. Betha had been offered the shower first, since she had less of it on her, which she appreciated. Somehow, she had escaped with no wounds, only a few bruises from the table pedestal to show for all the action that evening. Though the images inside her head weren't going to go away anytime soon, others hadn't walked away as easily.

He tried to protect me but was hurt. That can't happen again. I can't freeze. It doesn't matter if I am scared. And I can't be so useless next time. Goddess, I really hope there isn't a next time.

The shower turned off, and Betha scooted over in bed, closer to Joey. Thankfully it was a king bed and there was plenty of room. Still, she was going to be sleeping with other people. She and Angie had shared a bed before, but sharing with a dog and another guy moved this into territory well beyond her previous experience. Like, you only see this in late-night movies territory.

"You should be sleeping," Angie whispered softly to Betha before climbing into bed next to her.

"I know, but my brain won't shut up. I thought we were going to die, and then you came out of nowhere." Betha did her best to keep the wobble out of her voice.

Angie moved in closer, snuggling her. "I will always come and save your butt. That's what family is for. We all lived and walked away."

Betha said, "We were lucky that the portal had closed. If more of them had come through..."

"You can't look at what-ifs. It happened, we lived. Now is time for rest, then it will be time for planning and training. We can be prepared in case there is a next time. But right now, we need to get some sleep."

"I need to be a real Traveler, not just a human with a mark."

"Betha, it will all work out. You can start regular training tomorrow. You'll have to anyway since you're an Other now. Plus, I will be your first Anchor when you're ready, so don't worry about that."

Betha's mouth opened, but no words came out. She couldn't believe what Angie had just said. Becoming an Anchor was considered a huge honor. It was used as a status symbol during the Accords, but had downsides. It didn't always work, and people died. Well, those wanting to be an Anchor died. The Travelers seemed to end up okay. Betha had read about it, but still didn't really understand it, only knowing she had to have Anchors if she wanted to use her power, and that becoming an Anchor was for life and could be dangerous.

"It's late, and you don't need to decide tonight. We

both need our sleep," Angie continued into the silence. Angie pat her on her shoulder before rolling over.

"You would become my Anchor?" Betha finally whispered.

"Of course. Did you really think I wouldn't? Time to get some sleep. Plus, we don't want to wake Joey or Ben. The morning will come soon enough," Angie replied, and fell asleep.

Betha couldn't help the thoughts that were racing through her head. She didn't want things to change between her and Angie. Angie was all she had left. This wasn't something that staring at the ceiling was going to solve, and she did need to get some sleep. If only it was that easy. She had come to St. Luna's for the entrepreneurship program and to learn what she needed to so she could build a business, along with a legacy for her future family. Now that seemed so plain and so very far away. Money was less important when it seemed like the world was ending.

Joey started to whine again, and Betha rolled over on her side so she could keep stroking his back. His fur was so soft, and he made weird huffing noises as he slept. Tomorrow, things would make more sense. The rhythm of everyone slowly breathing eventually lulled Betha into a deep sleep.

It was too early in the morning, but Angie had promised to work out with her daily, and Betha needed it. Yesterday had been her first day working out, and she was still sore. She had always thought of herself as in reasonably good shape, but now she wasn't so sure. Angie had them both warm up with a light jog on the treadmills. Now covered in sweat, they were boxing, of all things. It was not going well. If this was like the twelve weeks of training all Others were required to get, she wasn't going to make it. Neither Betha nor Angie knew if she was going to be subject to the draft, and they had no idea who to ask. There were so few Travelers that there just wasn't any known precedent. Betha's advisor had reached out, and they had a meeting scheduled early Monday morning for "changes" to her schedule because of her status change.

Yesterday, there had been an all-school assembly about the attack in town. All the students except the shifters had attended. Angie hadn't even gotten an email about the assembly but went with Betha anyway. The whole presentation was along the lines of "if you see something, say something" and "campus is safe; stay on campus." Everyone in the crowd seemed to dismiss the incident—and the whole cautionary warning with it—as overblown.

Today was supposed to be a normal Sunday. Instead, Betha was running, boxing, and sweating.

"I don't think I am cut out for this," Betha gasped as she swung at the pad that Angie was holding up.

"It is your second day, girl," Angie said. "Today we are just building up muscle mass. We need to get you in better shape overall."

Given how much sweat was trickling down her back, Betha agreed. "I didn't think I was this out of shape. I run every day and do yoga."

"Both are a great base—it's just slower than what we are doing today. You got this!"

Betha was breathing hard, and she swore all the eyes in the gym were facing the mat that they were on. That wasn't the case, of course, and everyone was seriously working out with whatever they were doing, but Betha still felt self-conscious. It seemed that the gym was packed with people lifting weights, moving on machines, and sparring with each other. A few folks were superb, or at least they looked that way to her inexperienced eye.

She felt like she should have sounded the alarm or closed the portal—whatever that meant—to save a bunch of people in town. People died, and somehow, she might be able to stop that in the future. But she didn't know how much longer she could keep swinging at Angie. The heat on her back was intense, and the tremble in her arms frustrated her. If anyone had suggested that everything could change so quickly, Betha would have laughed. Never would she have pictured herself boxing in the gym with Angie. Maybe going for a run with her, or swimming, but not fighting.

I need to be stronger.

"I think we should wrap this up and stretch to cool down." Angie lowered the pads and motioned for Betha relax.

While Betha was thankful that Angie was pulling the plug on this session, she felt like she needed to resist. "I bet I can go for a bit more..." lied Betha. She might do more if she could, then pass out.

Angie shook her head. "No, we don't want to overdo it."

Betha resisted the urge to snap at Angie, even though she was right. This was just hard.

"Angie—who's your friend?" a new voice asked out of the general din.

Betha turned toward the male voice and couldn't help but stare. He was older than the two of them by a few years, but he was built like a truck. A beautiful truck. It took everything Betha had to not start blushing, and even then, she wasn't sure she succeeded.

Angie motioned to introduce the two of them. "Hey Carter. This is Betha. I was hoping to run into you today. Can you help put together a training program for her?"

Carter's blue eyes traveled over Betha, his eyebrows pulled together. He gave her a quick once-over, then shrugged. "Betha, your friend from back home? I only work with the Guard—you know that." His eyes flickered back to Betha. Betha was sure she was turning red by the moment. The hot guy was checking her out. She couldn't help the blush. Add in that she was covered in sweat and trying to not tremble, and it was a lost cause.

"Yeah, she is family, and it turns out, the new Traveler. Just completely human at the moment."

His eyes softened as he caught Betha's gaze. "Well, in that case, you know I'll help. I bet I'll get the order by tomorrow, anyway." He held his hand out to Betha. "Carter, as Angie mentioned. I'm also human, but in the Guard. I can help get you into fighting shape. You'll have to get through the mandatory training period."

Betha shook his hand and did her best not to drool. Once she let go, she turned toward Angie. "Wait, I thought you were going to train me?" Betha asked, the confusion in her voice.

"I can only get you so far. Carter is the best at what

he does. I don't know how to press you; you are family, after all. He won't care about that. All that matters to Carter is that you are the best you can be. That you can save others and stay alive doing it."

His laughter rolled over both of them. "Seems some of my lessons wore off on you after all, Angie. Betha, send me a text and I will craft you a schedule. Don't be late." He turned toward another person who was entering the gym and waved. It seems they were dismissed. Angie grabbed her phone and sent Betha his number.

"Let's go shower, but we need to make it quick—Grandpappy is here," Angie said.

"Wait, what? Already?"

Betha wasn't sure how many more surprises she could take today. First meeting Carter, who was her new personal trainer, and now she was going to get some firsthand information about Anchors. Maybe she'd even figure out a little bit about what she was supposed to do now.

"Yeah, he texted me. They both are here. He brought his Traveler."

Scratch that, Anchors *and* Travelers. Information overload. Betha paused while walking out of the gym. "That was fast."

Angie shrugged. "Come on, we both need showers, and we don't want to be late. Carter and Grandpappy both hate people being late—they have that in common."

CHAPTER NINE

Betha, freshly showered in record time, walked with Angie toward Pack Hall. There were conference rooms in the basement, and that was where they were meeting. They had both walked quickly back to Angie's room to shower fast and change since, as Angie put it, they both "smelled like sweaty socks." The sunlight felt really good on Betha's face, and she was glad that Angie knew where they were going. Campus seemed like a big place, though this area was more focused on the administration side of things. Pack Hall was a giant building, and Betha admired the stained-glass windows. She followed Angie around a corner and down a set of steps. The glass doors to the basement area were closed but unlocked. They led to a carpeted hallway of doors.

"You are thinking so hard I can feel it! It'll be fine—you know Grandpappy." Angie smiled at Betha and checked the room number. She knocked before she opened the door and motioned Betha inside. Immediately, Betha was wrapped in a hug that smelled of cigarettes and pine trees.

"Grandpappy!" Betha exclaimed, her head buried in his shirt, before pulling back from the embrace. As she looked at him, Betha realized he hadn't aged a day since she was five years old when she'd him. He still had that look of an older cowboy with a short white beard. The crinkles around his eyes spoke of the humor he held in check and the smile that often ghosted across his weathered face. As his large arms relaxed their hold, Betha couldn't remember a time his broad, solid presence hadn't brought a peace to the space around him.

He let her go and straightened up, then wrapped Angie in a hug as well. "It is not every day I get to see the two of you. It has been too long, though that means that both of you haven't gotten into trouble, so I guess that's okay." Whenever Angie had gotten in trouble or run away, it was always Grandpappy who brought her back. "I have someone that I want you both to meet." He motioned them toward a woman sitting at the conference table.

Betha turned on a smile and paused. The woman looked similar to her mother. Her eyes were the same hazel, along with the jawline. Yet, there were differences too. She seemed younger than her mother, and her hair was a different shade of brown. Grandpappy said something, but she didn't hear it.

"Betha?" Angie touched her hand to get her attention.

"Sorry, I missed that," answered Betha. "You look like my mom," she blurted out to the stranger.

The Traveler stood and held out her hand. "My name is Kyra, and I am pretty sure I am your great aunt, a few times removed. There aren't many of us Travelers. We all tend to be related somehow. I didn't mean to startle you." Kyra motioned to two of the chairs at the table near the door. "How about we take a seat?"

Grandpappy motioned to the couch on the other side of the room. "Angie, let's give them some space to talk." Angie gave Betha a smile but moved away, leaving her alone with Kyra. Well, as alone as they could be with two shifters in the room. Betha knew they would hear every word.

Betha took a seat at the table as Kyra had indicated, and the other Traveler sat across from her. Betha couldn't help but stare. The older woman could be her aunt if they were judging by looks alone. "James tells me you had no clue about being a Traveler, that your mother didn't speak of it," Kyra said. It took a moment for Betha to remember that James was Grandpappy's actual name.

"I knew nothing about it until I went to the health center to get my mark looked at. Someone had suggested it was a sunspot. My mom is at Luna's Grace. The nurse said something about a curse." Betha knew she was just babbling, the information all tumbling together, but Kyra seemed to accept it.

The older Traveler rolled her eyes. "It isn't really a curse; it is a choice that each of us needs to make. Most people don't understand what we are. Which is a good thing, to tell the truth. There aren't many of us near Terra, and if people really understood how we do what we can do, they would want to control us. Our bloodlines are connected to the leylines, which are the living lines of force that bind the universe together. The portals are doorways, passages to other worlds via the leylines. As a Traveler, it's easy to lose yourself in leylines. It's one reason we have Anchors—they ground us so we don't lose parts of our souls to the Universe."

"Why didn't my mom have Anchors, then? It sounds like people find it an honor to be an Anchor." Frustration at her mother was building. It was because of her she was in this spot, not knowing who or what she was. And maybe her mom had made the choice that had taken her away so suddenly, which might be the most painful thing of all.

Kyra paused before responding. "Who knows? It was a choice that she made. Being a Traveler isn't the easiest path that the fates can give to someone. Dealing with portals is dangerous work. Even being Anchored isn't always enough, plus you can lose an Anchor. No one lives forever, and losing anchors is painful beyond typical grief." She tapped on the table a few times. "I guard the Nexus here on Terra. It is a grouping of portals, but I can't leave it for long, or the portals will become unstable. I created the Nexus, bringing together the various portals on this world from all of the far-off locations where they would naturally reside. It's why everyone signed the Accords, which created the council, and that has brought Terra peace and prosperity. It was the right choice, but the cost is my freedom to travel."

Betha hadn't realized that Kyra was literally the one who had created the Nexus. She had learned about the Nexus in school, vaguely, and how it had stopped the war with the elves and the fey. The Accords were a treaty that kept Earth from being invaded by other species through the portals and created the first council. Representatives of the different species sat on the council and governed Terra. It was led by the human representative. Being the one who created the Nexus meant that Kyra was much older than Betha thought.

"Wait, how old are you?" The question slipped out before Betha could stop herself.

"Older than I look. Probably older than your mother. We each need to make our own choices. Maybe that was your mother's goal. Be a mom." Kyra's voice softened. "Raising a family as a Traveler usually isn't done. Normally, the child is given up to be raised by their partner, close friends or their Anchor families since they are doing their duty. They remain hidden while they are young and learn how to use their power safely." Kyra leaned back in her chair. "Your mother must not have wanted that. You can't fault her for making that choice. I know I can't."

Betha couldn't believe that Travelers didn't raise their own kids. That wasn't her life. Her mom had been there every step of the way until after high school. Until her memory went. It didn't explain why her mother didn't get an Anchor or teach her about being a Traveler and what it meant. And now she couldn't ever ask.

"Still, she didn't tell me anything," whispered Betha.

Kyra reached out and patted her hand awkwardly. "More than likely, she meant to tell you about all of this, but she had already started to lose herself. She wouldn't have even realized it had happened. One of the first things to go is the knowledge about what we are. It is an odd twist of fate."

Betha nodded slowly. She had tried more than once in that last summer to get her mother to remember who she was and that Betha was her daughter. It made sense that her mother might have meant to share these things, but she had run out of time. Still, it didn't reduce the pain or frustration Betha felt at her lack of knowledge.

"So, what happens to me now?" Betha asked. That frustration crept into her voice. She was twenty-one, looking forward to building her life how she wanted. She had a plan, for heck's sake. Go to school, build a successful business, and have an amazing family. That all went out the window with a bang as she realized she had no idea what future a Traveler would have. And she knew she couldn't have a family and do to them what her mother's illness had done to her.

Kyra pulled her hand away. "That's up to you. You need to choose if you want to be a Traveler or not. If you do, you need to bond with an Anchor, and as you gain more Anchors, you gain abilities. Until then, you are pretty much human."

Betha shook her head slowly. "Well, not completely human. The night of the attack in town, I heard buzzing in my head and my mark hurt."

Kyra looked puzzled, then smoothed her expression. "You must be sensitive then, but without an Anchor, you can't do much. An Anchor will keep your soul from getting caught in the leylines."

Betha pushed her chair back a little. "My mother

wasn't messing with the leylines. Why did she lose her memory? I don't understand how this works."

"Sorry, I am trying to give you a crash course. Your magic is going to reach out to the leylines no matter how hard you resist. They are a part of what you are. Over time, you will lose yourself, bits of your soul. I have always been Anchored, so I haven't lost anything. But being without an Anchor, it will happen. It always does."

"But what does a Traveler actually *do*? You somehow moved portals from around the world to create the Nexus. You closed the portal that opened downtown." Betha felt more confused than when this conversation had started. Everything she had read had been very vague. It was like no one knew or wanted to say anything about Travelers. Now here was an actual Traveler, and it didn't feel like she knew anything more. Betha only had more questions.

Kyra took a deep breath. "Travelers and the leylines are connected. Portals are just where the lines connect to a world. They create pathways from one world to another. We keep them stable. Downtown wasn't a portal—that was a tear. Things usually don't happen like that." A beeping sound came from her pocket, and Kyra quickly silenced it. "Once you are Anchored, if that is your choice, we can dig into this more."

It still felt like Betha was missing something about not being Anchored. "So how do I become Anchored then? How do I pick a good Anchor? I don't want to lose parts of me."

A knowing smile came over Kyra's face, and she leaned across the table. "An Anchor isn't good or bad.

They offer their magic and part of their soul to serve the Traveler. You don't need to spend time with them. They serve you, and you are in service to the leylines. In my case, I bonded with several people to cement the Accords. It tied all of us together for a time and helped stabilize things after the war."

"But how do you bond with an Anchor?"

Kyra reached for Betha's hand, and when they touched, warmth filled Betha's palm. "Feel that?" Betha nodded. "You need to touch them and reach out with that warmth. It is your power."

"That's it?" It sounded too easy. Way too easy for the type of life-changing moment it would be.

"That's the only part you control. From there, it is up to the goddesses of fate to create the bond. After that, you need to figure out the bond you have with your Anchor. It is different in every circumstance. It is a relationship, a mutual choice, and while it cannot be undone, it is also always unique."

Kyra removed her hand, but not before Betha noticed Kyra's wrist. Lines covered the inside of her wrist, extending up under her sleeve. Her mark was definitely much more intricate than Betha could have imagined. Betha could feel the warmth coming from her own palm now. "It's the same way you close a tear in the lines. You focus the power in your hand and use it to close the tear. You are a conduit of the leylines. You just give it instructions."

"A warm palm is my magic power?" deadpanned Betha.

Kyra laughed and shook her head. "I haven't heard it

described as such before, but I guess, in a way, that's accurate. One of the reasons people will want to bond with you is we live a very long time. Longer than any of the species on Terra, and so do our Anchors. Keep that in mind—you have time. Anyway, I don't make the rules, but the honest truth is no one who wants the portals to work would dare hurt you. Without us, they aren't stable."

"I have no idea what's going on."

"Unfortunately, that's how it works," replied Kyra. "Being a Traveler is different for each of us, and we each need to make our own way. There aren't many of us on Terra. Speaking of—I need to head back to the Nexus. With these tears, it's taking more and more energy to keep it stable."

Betha stood as Kyra did, smiling at the older Traveler. "Tears?" asked Betha. Her brain was fried with all the information, but now she knew what she was and what her powers actually meant. Well, sort of.

"Nothing for you to worry about right now. You should visit after you bond with your first Anchor. I will show you how the Nexus works," replied Kyra

"That sounds good. Thanks for coming to speak with me. I really appreciate it," said Betha.

"Of course. We are sort of related. Plus, if I hadn't, I wouldn't have been here to close that tear downtown on Friday." Kyra smiled at her and started toward the door.

Angie came up behind Betha and placed an arm around her shoulders. "You okay?"

Betha nodded. She still couldn't get over how Kyra

had looked so much like her mother. She wondered if all Travelers had similar looks.

"Yeah. Where did Grandpappy go?" Betha noticed he was no longer in the room.

"He is taking Kyra back. It was good to see him. Did you find out what you needed?"

Betha nodded again, feeling like a bobblehead. "I guess. Maybe everything sounded very simple, but I am guessing she was trying to not scare me with all of this. I wish I had heard it from my mom." *I wish I could ask her now.* She hung her head a little, but focused on Angie and moving forward, since that's all she could do.

CHAPTER TEN

Kyra closed the door behind her, feeling James' eyes burning into her back. His anger and frustration were apparent within their bond.

She turned around, leaning up against the wall, feeling as old as she really was. All four hundred years, and it felt like all of them were catching up with her. Betha was so very young. Traveler children were usually hidden and taught what they were as they aged. She was still a baby, and she didn't even know it. For one to pop up out of nowhere, the daughter of another Traveler who had taken no Anchor, was unheard of. Until now.

Kyra did not know how it was even possible. She was going to have to reach out to the one Traveler she was still in contact with to see if they knew anything about Josephine or Betha. All Kyra currently knew was that Josephine had appeared out of nowhere with Betha in her arms when Betha was barely a year old. Before that, there was nothing, and she had everyone digging into records. Not to mention, how did Josephine get here without Anchors? Travelers couldn't use the portals without one.

"You didn't give Betha too much to go on there. Pour your power into your hand, and that's how you close the tears. Really?" James stared at her, his eyes glowing softly.

"Andrea said to keep it as simple as possible—give her the basics, don't deep dive, and everything would work out correctly." Her own frustration escaped her lips as she added, "You know how it is. Andrea has not steered us wrong yet with her visions."

"Yeah, but she didn't warn me that Angie was going to be part of this. She is my bunny—why does she need to be an Anchor?"

"Come on, James, you know better than to ask that question. She was born to be an Anchor, just like you were. Your bunny brought you back to civilization after a long century away, and now it's her turn to help a new Traveler. Angie is a shadow wolf. You had to know when she changed that she would not have a normal life. Betha is saving her from being turned into the council's assassin or popping out babies every year. Or both, goddess help her. Instead, she will be an Anchor with a destiny. She is escaping her life with style. You should be happy for her!"

Kyra threw her arms up, but she understood where James was coming from. Betha was related to her somehow, and if she had known that Betha's mother had made the choices she had, Kyra would have stepped in.

Given that Andrea had said nothing to her about Betha, Betha needed to be right where she was. It was hard being friends with a seer. Always having to do the right thing, even if it hurt.

"You know I don't like this any better than you do. Betha did not know she was a Traveler, and we have no idea what world she or her mother showed up from. If your bunny didn't know you were an Anchor, we wouldn't have been here to close that tear. Think about that and all of those demons in town."

James grit his teeth, doing his best not to hit something. Kyra knew he understood but it didn't mean he had to be happy about it. Watching your many-times-removed children grow up had been easier for him than watching his own kids grow up. Most times it had been hard for him to connect with his extended family, but not bunny. Angie had dragged him out of his cabin in the woods and reconnected him with his descendants. When she had shifted the first time, he left his cabin and hadn't gone back. Kyra had been thankful.

Now they both knew why he had connected with her so much. She was a chip off the old block, a very old block in both their cases. Hopefully, she would not follow in all of his footsteps, only the better ones.

"Andrea is going to hear from me," growled James.

"She already knows that. It's exactly what she wants. Her days are numbered, and she needs to line everything up." Kyra met his eyes head-on, which was something she rarely did. You never looked an alpha wolf in the eyes. Few could and survive. But Kyra showed no fear because she was not afraid.

James froze at those words. “That’s not possible... you mean—”

“According to Andrea, it is happening, and we need to make sure it happens correctly. This might be the last hurrah. You might get your peace after this. We both might finally be done with this mess.”

CHAPTER ELEVEN

"Again!"

Heck.

Betha pulled herself up from the floor and did her best not to flinch. Most of her time was spent on the floor of the gym. At least there were mats. Joey was across from her and hadn't offered a hand up. He was her opponent during these sessions with Carter. Betha quickly learned training was always serious with Carter. He treated training like it mattered, and he loved the fact that he had two new recruits. It turned out Joey had delayed his basic training, and now he had to face the music as well.

Joey stayed in his golden lab form for two days before changing back. When he did change back, his eyes were darker, and he held himself differently. Being attacked had changed him, and it didn't feel like a good thing. He didn't seem to chatter as much anymore, and there were no puppy dog eyes in sight. Now they were being pitted against one another, and it wasn't fun. Then again, she knew this would never be fun. Fighting wasn't something she wanted to get better at, it was something she had to do. It did not come naturally to her at all, but to protect herself and others, she would try her best.

Joey raised his fists and darted at her. She was supposed to be dodging and not letting him touch her. Betha dodged but didn't see the other fist before she was on the floor. At least he was pulling his punches. She wasn't sure that she could take many of his hits at full strength.

"Let's do this slower. Joey, half speed," called out Carter.

Betha got up off the mat again, took another breath to center herself, and slowly dodged the punch, raising her hand to push it to the side. This was basic, but she kept getting lost in her head or the look on Joey's face. It was like he wasn't home. It bothered her that he could just shove everything aside, yet for her, everything was still terrifying. If an attack happened again, she needed to be ready to do her job, and the pressure was mounting.

The training lasted another forty minutes, and Betha was so happy when it was finally done. She slumped to the bench and grabbed her water bottle.

"You are getting better," Carter said as he sat down next to her. Thankfully, she no longer blushed when Carter was close. It had taken a few days before she could ignore the fact that he was hot, but she still lusted after him. "It takes time. You need to build the memory in your body to move without thinking about it. All that matters is your goal. Tomorrow is 'king of the hill.' Your goal is to get to the flag—nothing else matters. You get to the flag, and the portal closes. After you get the flag, you dodge. You don't let them touch you. Let the team take care of the enemies. Make sure you get some good sleep tonight."

"Got it. Keep moving, get to the flag, then don't let them get me after the fact," answered Betha.

"Exactly." Carter gave her a smile, and she felt butterflies in her stomach. "Plus, you need to get through the basic twelve weeks like everyone else." He patted Joey on the shoulder as he got up and headed to the next group he was working with.

Betha grabbed her bag and shuffled around in it. "Hey, Joey?"

He turned those horrible eyes her way.

"I was wondering if you wanted to play ball with me?" She pulled a new tennis ball out of her bag and held it up to him. Joey's lips parted, and his eyes grew wide. A spark flickered across his face, and his mouth closed.

"I mean, it was a dumb idea. I thought it would be relaxing after all of this." Betha turned away, but he reached out and touched her shoulder.

"You would really play ball with me?" he asked quietly.

She turned back and nodded. "I wasn't joking. Angie and I used to play—those were some of my best memories during the summer."

"I would love to play. Let me drink some water, then meet you out front?" For the first time since the attack, he looked like himself. His eyes were brighter. That was something that mattered, more than Betha had thought it would.

Betha smiled. "Sounds good!" She practically bounced toward the door of the gym, her aching shoulders forgotten. It didn't take long for a large golden lab to make its way out of the building with its tail wagging. Betha tossed the ball across the lawn before he got all the way to her, and she watched as he darted out after it.

Joey was even a good sport, dropping the ball at her feet to throw again. "This one is going to go far!" Betha continued tossing the ball for Joey. Watching him dart about was such a relief. This was why she kept going to training sessions and why she tried so hard. Moments of the sun shining, a shifter barking, and hanging out with her friends. Betha snapped a picture of Joey running across the field toward the ball and sent it to Angie. She would enjoy the shot.

~

Betha hated "king of the hill." Well, "king of the field." The field in question had several trees in it for cover but was mostly open and flat. She had "died" so many times now she had lost count. Sometimes she had made it to the flag that stuck out from a tree limb—the fake portal she needed to get to with her team—but closing it had only happened once. She really wished that Angie was here, yet she had a different schedule.

The team had tried a few different approaches, but she could tell that some shifters were getting frustrated.

Betha didn't know how to solve the problem and was thrilled when Carter called time.

"Who can tell me what keeps going wrong?" No one spoke up, and Carter glared at folks. Finally, someone spoke up. Everyone was sitting, or in Betha's case, lying in the grass.

"It's too easy to take out the Traveler. Not with a gun, but the other team knows who she is and what she is trying to do. When they focus on her, we fail."

Carter nodded. "Anyone else?"

"It's easy to take her down," muttered someone from the group, quietly enough that Betha couldn't identify them. She knew it was true, and she felt bad about it even though she wasn't ever going to be as strong or as fast as shifters. Four shifters plus her against five other shifters wasn't a winning strategy.

"I need an Anchor." Betha shocked herself by speaking up from the grass. "Right now, I am the only human on that battlefield, and I can't keep up. I am smaller, slower, and easy to target." Her words seemed to cause several people to shuffle about and avoid her gaze.

It was a so-called honor to be an Anchor, and Betha knew there were several folks who were aiming for the position as her first. The more Betha read about the last time Kyra had taken Anchors, the more upset she got. It was used as a status symbol and had gotten certain families chosen to lead their people. Add in a long life and the potential political power, and it made it so she didn't know who to trust.

Both people had to be committed to the bond though, or it wouldn't happen, and the potential Anchor could die. Betha had read what research she could find, and the survival stats were pretty horrible. Someone couldn't be forced to be an Anchor, and a Traveler had to choose, really choose with their whole heart and soul, to accept the power and the responsibility that came with it. Because a piece of the Anchor's soul was transferred to the Traveler, it was a major event, and it could not be reversed. If the Traveler's soul rejected them, the Anchor could die. On the flip side, if it all went well, the Traveler would share in the new Anchor's abilities, though it wasn't clear what form they would take.

Carter smiled at Betha. "I want all of you to think about that before we play again later this week. Betha, one moment, if you please."

Betha peeled herself off of the ground and headed toward Carter, dodging folks who were heading to the showers. "Yeah?" she said as she sat next to him.

"You are doing good and showing improvement. Don't use this as an excuse to rush to bond with someone."

"I know I can't rush it. It's just frustrating being human in a field of shifters. They are literally faster and stronger than I can ever be as a human."

"Believe me, I know. It can be hard, but you will also learn from it. Look at me." He tapped his chest. "I am a human in the Guard. The head trainer to boot."

"How did you let it not get to you?" Betha couldn't help but look at some shifters who were jogging around the track next to the field.

"I focused on my strengths. I can build teams that work—most Others are too tribal to work well across different species types. I practiced until I could outshoot them. I know everything I can about the strengths and weaknesses of Others. Yes, my teammates are faster, but I am smarter. I have also spent more time training, and I know to not get caught in a hand-to-hand fight with someone who can beat me. I turn the situation to my advantage. You need to look at your strengths and use them."

"That sounds like so much work," sighed Betha.

Laughter started rolling out from Carter.

"At least one of us thinks this is funny," she said a little bitterly.

Carter patted her on the back. "You have Anchors for a reason, and you are the only one who can do what you do. Keep practicing calling your power. The more you know about yourself, the better. Practice the meditation sessions that I assigned. An Anchor will happen when it happens. Until then, getting you in the best physical and mental shape possible is key."

Betha nodded. "I am now in the best shape I have ever been." She knew it was true, but she also knew that she wasn't done. She had a long way to go before she was the best she could be.

"You need to keep in mind, King of the Hill isn't about you—it's about them. They are used to fighting and training together, but that doesn't help when they are assigned to a team with folks who aren't shifters. They need to learn how to work with others and protect members of their team with different strengths and weaknesses from them. Pack tactics work, but when you throw a non-shifter like a witch or a healer on the team, things don't go as smoothly. Right now, they are working with a team they have worked with their whole lives. You are a first to them."

"I didn't think of that." Betha asked the one question she had been wondering about. "Why isn't Angie assigned to my group?"

A grim line crossed Carter's face. "The powers that be have different plans for Angie, and that is outside of my control." He really looked at her face. "It might not be out of yours though." Carter stood and ruffled her hair. "No matter what, you got this, kiddo."

Betha's eyes bugged at the word kiddo. "Hey, I am not that much younger than you. You have what, eight years on me?" She did not want Carter to see her in a kid light. Not at all.

"You're, what, nineteen, if that?" asked Carter.

Betha winced. "More like twenty-one. Turning twenty-two in a few months."

"Oh, sorry. You look younger."

"It's a Traveler thing. We age slowly." Which was an understatement. From what she could tell, she would stop aging in her late twenties. After that, it wasn't clear how long she would live. It was one benefit of becoming an Anchor since your life was defined, at least in part, by your Traveler.

Carter set a hand on her shoulder. "I didn't realize it was such a sore subject. I'm sorry."

Betha blushed when she realized how transparent her emotions had been. "It's all good. In a few decades, it will be a good thing. Everyone always wants to look young once they hit thirty."

Carter laughed. "I'll let you know in a couple of years when the big one hits. Anyway, get some rest tonight."

Betha was walking back to her dorm when she realized what Carter had said. The council had plans for Angie, and she hadn't even asked her friend what was going on. Plans that, from the sound of it, weren't what Angie wanted. She would have to get her friend to spill and find some way to help.

CHAPTER TWELVE

It was as normal a day as Betha could have expected, given all that was going on. Her schedule had drastically changed since her first week of school. Instead of her business classes, now she was going to extra classes on the Others. Everything one normally learned at an Others' middle and high school she was now having to learn at a blistering rate. The only class that was the same was her economics class. It didn't seem that she would graduate with a degree anytime soon. On the bright side, all the extra classes were being paid for by the council. Since these were required, they were free, just like the training.

The schooling was in addition to the training sessions she had almost every afternoon. Carter was hard on her, but she had to admit she needed it. As Angie had warned, her training with him was completely different. He could push her right up to her absolute limits and then show her she could move a little bit past them every time.

Her class schedule wasn't the only thing that had changed. Every which way she turned on campus, Betha would see Guard members patrolling with junior Pack members. The Guard was the only military force on Terra. Some of the species had their own police forces for their lands, like the Pack, but the Guard took care of everything else. The local news had covered the portal opening near the nightclub, and Betha had discovered this wasn't the only occurrence of it happening. Demons had sprung up in several locations, and fighting was going on around the globe. Her own high school classes had taught that this was what the Nexus and the Accords were supposed to prevent, but somehow, things weren't going well.

Saint Luna's was mostly an Others' school. One of the best, in fact, but even still, most of her human classmates had paused taking classes or gone to online only. War protocol was put into place by the council. All she knew about it was that the draft had been called. All adult Others under a certain age were subject to the draft and had to train with the Guard just in case. The Guard had always had enough members in the past who volunteered and signed up. The benefits were good, and if you enlisted with the guard once you were done with basic training, you were free of any additional draft requirements once your contract was over with. Still, if you hadn't volunteered and were Other, you could be drafted if needed. The draft hadn't been called in her memory, until now.

Given her quasi-changing state, she only knew that she needed to report to Carter and that she wasn't being drafted. Or at least, she wasn't being drafted yet. Angie was already drafted, along with most of the Others left on campus. Everyone else had gone home almost overnight, and classes had moved to entirely remote learning. Even knowing they had trained a lot longer and harder than she had didn't stop Betha from worrying about Angie or Ben.

Her housing situation was also weird. She had gotten the notice she needed to pack her stuff and move to a different part of campus by the end of the week. It was unclear where her new room was, but she hoped it was closer to her friends. When she was free, her time was spent with Angie. Today it was raining, so they were at Angie's place sitting at her small dining table.

Betha snorted to herself. So much could change in two weeks. Just look—the world was getting invaded by demons from a different world, she was training with a very attractive older Guard member, her best friend had been drafted, and though Betha wasn't homeless, she was at least displaced.

"What are you laughing about?" asked Angie.

Betha glanced up from her homework at her friend, who was supposed to be working on some of her own. "Just how the goddess is laughing at us, and my situation."

"What? That you are kick-ass?" sassed Angie.

Betha couldn't help but roll her eyes. "You know what I mean." She stared at Angie until she looked back at her. "Were you serious about becoming an Anchor?" Betha asked quietly.

Angie set down her pencil and pushed her homework

to the side. "I was dead serious. We have been best friends forever, and you are a part of my chosen family. Plus, I think I would be an epic Anchor. I am not saying this to pressure you, but I have a feeling that if I don't become one, I am going to be sent out on missions soon." Angie looked a little worried at that last admission. "There is active fighting with demons going on that isn't really being reported, and they have already removed me from most of my classes. The powers that be let me keep my online drawing class, but I think that's just so I don't go completely ballistic on them."

Betha nodded her head slowly. "If you really mean that, then I think we should do this. Like, now, before I lose my nerve. I don't want to learn all of this Other stuff without you. Not to mention, maybe then I wouldn't get a random bodyguard assigned to me." The story of how bad she was at King of the Hill had been making the rounds across campus, though no one seemed to know that it was Betha the rumor was talking about. It seemed to be an unspoken rule—everyone said "the new Traveler" and not her name.

"Yeah, I volunteered for the spot along with Ben, but I was told that was unacceptable." Angie took a deep breath, then continued, "I spoke to Grandpappy about what happens, and the risks if I offered to be an Anchor."

Betha was slightly relieved. "At least you already know that you could die. I didn't know how to tell you that. It took me this long to ask because I really don't want to hurt you." Betha tried to smile, but the thought that she might kill her best friend was horrifying.

Angie tossed a highlighter at Betha. "I will not die.

This is where I am supposed to be. I know it, you know it, and soon everyone else will know it as well. We will do this. It doesn't matter what the council thinks—Travelers and their Anchors are above all of that. They aren't subject to the council rules."

"What does the council expect from you?" asked Betha softly.

Angie looked away from her and frowned. Her voice went quiet. "I can vanish when I am within a shadow. Like, I step into a tree shadow, and I am invisible. I am there but if someone tries to find me, I am not. It's hard to explain. Someday, I might be able to travel between shadows. The night wolves were assassins before they were wiped out, and supposedly once they grew into their powers, they could travel between shadows. Then, surprise! I manifest, and I am one, so I guess 'wiped out' isn't the right term." She turned back toward Betha with a rueful expression. "We both know that as things stand, I will be at their beck and call. The council is benevolent, generally, but they are mortals like the rest of us, and my power is tempting to use. My Alpha has already been really intense about who I date."

"So that's why you aren't dating Joey?"

Angie nodded her head.

"That doesn't matter if you become an Anchor, right? So let's just do it. We both know you will make an amazing Anchor for me." Betha moved over to the couch from the table, and Angie followed. "Watch this." Betha held out her palm, and light gathered slowly. The mark on her wrist glowed, and warmth spread out from her hand. "I have been practicing calling it up."

Angie leaned forward, her nose twitching. “Whoa, that's amazing.”

“Are you ready?” asked Betha, nerving herself up. She knew this was important, knew it was right, but also knew it was dangerous, and knew it was forever. But she had to do this—for herself, for Angie. She didn’t want to become like her mom; she wanted to help people, and live her life, with her best friend at her side.

Angie nodded. “Yes, let’s do this.”

Betha took another deep breath and placed her hand on Angie’s chest. It seemed right. Her voice came out strong, and it almost sounded like it was coming from every corner of the room. Her eyes gazed off into the distance, and Betha said the words almost without willing it, as though she were only observing something that was destined to be. “Angie, shadow wolf of the Saint Luna Pack, will you share your power and your soul? Will you accept and protect that which we will become? Will you be my Anchor?”

“Yes.” Angie answered in kind, her voice loud and proud.

A bright light flashed in the room from Betha’s hand, then everything went dark.

ANGIE WAS EXCITED. Today was chicken nugget day. Her mom called her a little carnivore, and she loved chicken nuggets. Steak was better, but the school cafeteria would not provide steak for the students. It was expensive.

Angie was also excited to tell Betha about Mary and

Jacob. Both were being transferred out. They had changed! It was amazing that people at their own school had changed. It didn't happen often in small towns, but each middle and high school was required to have an Other on staff who could recognize the warning signs. Not to mention control the newly manifested powers.

"Betha, you aren't going to believe it! Jacob is a werewolf and Mary is an elf person!"

Betha looked up at her best friend with a bright smile. Angie loved how Betha looked at her like she was the best thing to ever happen to her. They had been friends since they were really little, and they lived right next door to each other. Their back yards connected and everything.

Angie took her seat right next to her friend and set her tray down on the table. "Do you ever wonder about being Other?"

She watched as Betha set down her chocolate milk and grabbed a chicken nugget. "No, my mom says we have always been human in our family. Like as far back as records show. But that's okay."

Angie was listening to her friend. She really was, but Betha kept waving that chicken nugget in front of her. Like it was right there, and it smelled so good. She had to have the chicken nugget; Betha had to give it to her. It was *her* chicken nugget, and she was so hungry.

Betha's mouth fell open and her eyes went wide as she looked at Angie, who'd started to realize the whole room felt different. Colors were brighter, everything smelled stronger, and time seemed to slow. She reached for Betha's chicken nugget but then noticed the nails on her own hand had grown long and turned pitch black.

Carefully, Betha handed over the chicken nugget. "It's okay, Angie. You can have all the nuggets you want."

The cafeteria had been slowly cleared out by teachers, and Mr. Johnson the Watcher motioned for Betha to back away. She shook her head as Angie whined, realizing that something was wrong.

"Shh. It's okay Angie. I will always be your friend. Best friends forever." Betha closed her hand over Angie's clawed one and didn't react as Angie slumped forward, fainting.

CHAPTER THIRTEEN

It all made sense now, or at least it felt like it did. Betha was staring at the sunset, watching the orange turn pink and purple. She was shaken to her core, but in a good way. Before this week, she wasn't sure if she had faith—now it was a different story. Her faith in the goddess had gone up a notch or two.

She had placed a hand on her friend's chest, and now they were connected, bonded. It felt like part of her was left inside Angie. Or part of Angie was inside her. It wasn't clear. There had been flashes of a full moon and the sound of humming. Hopefully, it would make more sense as time went by. Even if she hadn't understood the process, it had worked.

"Friends forever, Traveler and Anchor." Betha smiled.

"You are thinking too hard." Angie joined her on the bench, staring over the forest at the darkening sky. "I hear the gears turning."

"It is so different now."

"But you don't regret it?"

"No, you know that."

Everything *was* different. The birds were so much louder. She took the stairs to the roof like it was nothing. Her movements were faster. Since she'd woken up that morning, her body was different, more fit. Not to mention the hunger.

Betha had slept for almost two days. Angie was thankfully up after one. While attempting the bonding on a Friday night had been a great idea, the weekend was almost over. This morning, three breakfast sandwiches didn't seem like a big deal, and it was only after the second sandwich that the hunger wasn't as sharp. The most visible change was her mark. Before, it was a dark star, but now it wasn't just a star anymore. It had shadows surrounding it, a star surrounded by black swirls of shadow or smoke.

The biggest change wasn't visible, though—Angie was inside her head. Betha received impressions from her, and vice versa. It wasn't like telepathy; they didn't read every thought or it would be maddening, but they could definitely sense each other. Betha knew, somehow, that this part of their bond would strengthen and focus over time, and she was glad of it. Now, she was never going to be alone.

Angie wrapped her arm around Betha's shoulder. "I know. We are both going to need to learn to not project, especially if we are fighting."

Betha nodded. "I'm trying, but I have a lot to learn. At least you already have a head start with that."

"I have been able to feel the Pack since middle school,

but it isn't, wasn't verbal. It isn't working well right now."

"What I don't understand is why you are worried," Betha tried to sound unconcerned but failed. "I know you have no regrets, yet you're worried."

Angie frowned a bit. "The Pack bond is strange. There is a separation with the Luna members now inside my head. It's like you took the spot that they were in. Justin will notice sooner rather than later, and I don't know what he'll say or do. I don't know if there's anything he *can* say or do." She turned to look directly at Betha. "And little did I know I was going to end up with a tattoo." Angie wiggled her eyebrows at Betha.

"What?"

"There is something on my chest, but I think it is still forming." She pulled her shirt down, and Betha could see a multi-pointed star, but she could swear it was moving, and the dark color seemed faded.

"That wasn't in the brochure. I thought shifters couldn't really get a tattoo?"

Angie shrugged her shoulders. "Once the Alpha finds out, this is going to change things. We need to talk to Carter tomorrow about all of this, and I need to talk to Justin before he finds out from someone else."

"You're acting like we won't be welcome here anymore." Angie didn't respond immediately, and Betha turned to look at her fully. "Now I *know* you are hiding something." Angie lowered her eyes, and Betha continued, "You can talk to me about anything. In fact, I think you had better, since now it impacts me too, whatever it is."

"It's hard to talk about since the Pack is the Pack. I am still part of it, but the biggest bond I have now is to you. I feel like I was always supposed to be your Anchor, like it was fate. Others wanted different things for me. I made a choice. It feels good. But that doesn't mean that the Alpha and the elders will be happy about losing their tool."

Betha completely understood, but part of her still wondered if being a Traveler was going to be a good or a bad thing. She knew this was the correct path. Now she had to walk down it with her head held high. After all, now that she had an Anchor, her choice had been made. It was time she said goodbye to the dreams she had. At least for the moment.

"What happened to you when you blacked out?" Angie asked.

"It is hard to describe. I could feel connections going to many places. I think it was the leylines. There was also a feeling of immense joy..." Betha trailed off and shook her head. "Words don't work for this," she mumbled. Instead, Betha tried to push the type of feeling she had gotten over to Angie.

"Whoa, what is this?" whispered Angie.

"Exactly. What about you?"

Angie opened her mouth, but she took a moment before speaking. "I went down memory lane. Nothing bad. Just things I had forgotten about." They both sat in a relaxed silence for a bit before Betha wondered about tomorrow. "Training tomorrow will be exciting. I can't wait to see what happens."

"You better not be late for Carter," teased Angie.

"I won't be," Betha thought back at her.

Betha's Monday morning started with a training session, and Angie tagged along without asking. In fact, Angie hadn't left her side since they had bonded, except when she had been sleeping it off or taking a shower.

"You know I can go places without you," Betha said as they headed toward the gym.

Angie shrugged. "I know you are an independent woman who can handle anything you put your mind to. But one word—demons. Reminder, they seem to be invading the world."

Betha didn't have a comeback to that one. She hadn't seen one since that night in the club, and that was a streak she wanted to continue. Last time she had seen a demon, people had died. Once in the gym, Betha headed to a treadmill to warm up. Her shadow followed. Everything was just like last week, except Angie was there. Once her run was done, she noticed Carter was chatting with another Guard. He gave her a smile and nodded when he saw Angie. His eyes flicked to her wrist, but otherwise, he said nothing. Instead, he jumped into training without skipping a beat, with instructions for them both.

"I don't think I can move," groaned Betha. She could feel the mat under her, along with the sweat-soaked tank top she was wearing. Her body hurt in all sorts of places. This workout had been several steps above and beyond what she normally did in the morning. More reps, more weights, and it had to be faster.

"Well, did you think that training was going to be easier with me by your side?" Angie's voice came up from the mat next to her. At least she wasn't the only one staring at the ceiling. Part of her was glad it hadn't only been hard for her. Though Angie's reps and weights had been higher than her own, that seemed only fair. She was the super powerful shifter, after all. Betha was only a lowly Traveler.

Carter hadn't seemed surprised at seeing Angie with her. In fact, he seemed pleased. Betha was trying her best to not think too hard about that. Though thinking was the only thing that didn't hurt at the moment. Well, it didn't hurt much, at least.

"Are you two going to remain on the mat all day?" asked Carter, standing over them.

Betha did her best to keep from rolling her eyes at Carter. She did not need another twenty-five pushups assigned. It was hard keeping her eyes off of him, so she focused on the ceiling. Her senses had increased enough that she could smell him. Betha swore his scent was pine needles and sunshine.

"I figured you would give me a bit more of a warm-up to get used to these unexpected changes," replied Betha.

"You thought wrong. The best way to get familiar with your changes is to use them. Let them soak into your body until it's normal. You both only have five more minutes, then it's on to the next round." Carter tossed a bottle of water near her head, but it didn't hit her. Betha gave a thumbs-up from the floor.

"He seems chipper," thought Betha at her new Anchor.

"I mean, it's Carter. He probably saw this coming days ago. The issue is going to be how Justin and the rest of the uppers see it. I spoke to Grandpappy about it, and he gave support. I probably should have spoken to Justin beforehand."

Betha sent back, *"Like you said, it is an honor to be asked."* She could hear Angie peeling herself off the floor, and Betha followed suit. It surprised her how quickly the ache was fading away.

"How tired are you?" asked Betha.

Angie shook her head. "Almost back to normal."

"I didn't get the full upgrade then. It's getting better fast, but not that quick."

A swig of water helped cool her down, and she was thankful for the improvements to her body that she got with Angie being an Anchor. She wasn't on Angie's level, but she was on a different scale than earlier this week. Sharing your soul with someone had some perks.

A group of shifters followed Carter as he made his way back over to the two of them. "It is going to be two on three. Angie, your goal is to stop them from taking down Betha. Betha, you need to touch the far wall." Carter took a few minutes going over the rest of the rules.

"Can you take the three of them?" Betha asked Angie.

"Maybe. You should be able to get to the wall. Actually, head for the switch behind you first."

The whistle went off, and Angie shifted into her wolf

form, tearing her clothes. Betha took off toward the wall at an angle, the light switch in her sight. She could hear Angie struggling with the shifters.

"One on your tail!"

Betha hit the switch, and the room fell into darkness. Angie would be exponentially harder to see in the dark. Two additional shifters joined the fight when Carter blew the whistle, but Betha slowly made her way across the room to the far wall, brushing her fingers against it. Then the lights were back on, and Carter was standing next to the light switch.

"That was a good use of strategy," he said.

All five shifters were on the floor, and Angie was still in her wolf form. She smiled as much as a wolf can smile. Betha could feel her satisfaction and amusement. Maybe this would work out even better than she had hoped.

CHAPTER FOURTEEN

Betha's excitement was apparent. Now that it felt like she was caught up on the basics of being an Other, it was time to learn more about being a Traveler and the actual portals. Kyra had invited her to see the Nexus, and Betha hoped to learn more than she had the first time she'd met the older Traveler. Even if she didn't, leaving campus would be a nice change. The last time she'd been off campus, demons had attacked. This time, she felt more prepared, and hopefully demons wouldn't attack. Either way, some new scenery would be welcome.

After meeting Angie, Betha expected to grab a cab or take a bus. Instead, Angie led her to an obscure stairwell leading down into nothingness. It was next to the library on campus, and as they approached, Betha knew something was different about it. She could feel it, and her mark buzzed. Betha was confused as Angie led the way down into the darkness.

"Are you sure this is the place? How are we going to get a cab down here?" asked Betha.

Angie kept moving down into the darkness. "Yep, this is the place. We aren't taking public transit. It's not safe enough anymore. We just have one more doorway to go."

Betha kept up with Angie and strained her ears to see if she could hear anything ahead. It was then that she realized how quiet the grim space was. Angie stepped through an archway into a larger chamber, and as Betha followed, she realized the archway was, again, special.

"Do you feel that?" asked Betha.

Angie immediately paused and glanced at her. "Feel what?"

"The doorway was different, and this was as well."

"Shit, I didn't think to warn you—they are shortcuts. I don't know the official name, but they connect two places on Terra that aren't too far apart. We have one that leads up near the mountains, as well. This one comes out around forty-five minutes away."

Betha nodded her head, thinking about what her friend had said. They must be like portals, but she'd had no idea such things existed. Less like portals, and maybe more like ripples since portals connect two works and these connect two places on the same world. Angie continued moving forward. As soon as Betha stepped through, she found herself in a large open building with people bustling back and forth through different doors. She couldn't keep track of what she was seeing. It was bright, and Betha realized it was more like a courtyard rather than a building. There wasn't a roof. Everything seemed to be very old and a little dusty. Rough stone covered the floor and the various archways that led away. And the people. So many different types and races of people. There were some she recognized, but many she had no idea about. Off the top of her head, she could point out the trolls—taller than the rest—along with what looked to be smaller trolls, but their skin wasn't green. The shifters were an everyday occurrence for her, but there were lots of other beings as well.

As she looked closer, she realized some of these folks must be fey. Satyrs, and beings with wings like butterflies, along with other variations. The crowds moved back and forth along one direction, and that was the way Angie headed. Angie realized Betha had slowed down and grabbed her hand.

"That was the shortcut to the council lands. Now we just need to head to the Nexus. Keep up. You don't want to get pick pocketed here. Yes, there are lots of different people, but this isn't anything—just wait."

That Angie had answered her questions before she even asked them was a blessing and a curse. They were getting used to being in each other's heads, but Betha hadn't realized how the lack of privacy would get to her. She figured she didn't have any secrets from Angie, so it wouldn't matter. But it did matter, and it was definitely taking some adjustment. For Angie, it was different. She had been with the Pack for long enough that sharing some level of surface thoughts was second nature. Still, it had its upsides, and being able to make sure Betha didn't look too confused in public was one of them.

They turned a corner, and suddenly there was a

marketplace. Betha stopped walking and stared. Angie let go of her hand and paused, giving her time to look around. The area was the size of a football field, and different vendors had stalls spread around seemingly at random. Some had normal folding tables and plastic white tents over them. Others had to be from far away places, or different worlds. Brightly colored cloth tents, carpets, and was that a donkey with fangs?

No one gave them a second glance. The place was thick with people of all shapes and sizes. The variety of other species was amazing. There were too many to label, and people she had only imagined from books, like dwarves, pixies, and beings made entirely of smoke she had no name for. The chatter was almost overwhelming, only some of which she understood. The stall nearest to her was selling glittering cloth. Pixies haggled with customers, who looked to be dwarven.

The smell of many different roasted meats filled the air, and something covered with red hair turned a spit over a fire. Humans stood around it waiting to be served. Though, Betha realized, they probably weren't human, given where they were. They might be witches, or healers, or something else that she didn't know about.

"Time to get moving," said Angie.

Giant doorways framed a central building, and one bright blue one caught Betha's eye. She felt drawn to it. It wasn't solid—it was more like it was made of light. They slowly made their way down the largest walkway that led directly to the blue, shimmering door.

"Grandpappy gave me a rundown of where to go. He should...there he is!" Angie said, almost to herself.

Grandpappy walked out of the blue door. His face lit up at seeing Angie, and Betha couldn't help but smile as well. He wrapped his arms around both girls, giving them a squeeze.

"It's good you both are here. Kyra is inside. Come on."

He headed back inside the open door, and Betha realized that there were armored Guards on either side. She hadn't noticed them until she had passed through the bright blue light.

Kyra approached Betha with a smile. "It's good to see you again so soon, and congratulations are in order." The older woman looked between the two of them. "Bonding with your first Anchor is special, a cause to celebrate. Maybe after I show you around, we will take you both out to dinner." A look passed between Grandpappy and Kyra, but Betha couldn't guess what it meant. She couldn't help but wonder if they were talking like she did with Angie. Yet, somehow, she really didn't want to ask.

Kyra nodded at the Guards on either side of the door, and they left through the bright blue light. The door darkened until it was a solid object. "Since you are bonded now, we can speak freely together. This is the Nexus." Kyra's hands motioned to the room they were in.

Betha looked around and noticed that there were several archways in the walls of the room. It was a giant circle with different colored doors. They were like the archways on the outside of the building. After looking around with her eyes, she reached out with her power. Betha could feel sparks of power in each of the doorways. Somehow, she could sense that they all led to different worlds.

"Whoa," she muttered, stunned.

"I wondered if you could feel them. I have used my power to move the different portals to this location. While it limits how far away I can travel, my choice to keep them here has provided a host of benefits to Earth. Like the market outside, along with being a neutral location for different worlds to meet."

Angie spoke up, "This was how you brokered the peace between the various worlds? You forced everyone to sign the Accords, or their world wouldn't be on the Nexus?"

Betha paused her review of the different doors, walking among them, and turned to face Kyra, really looking at her. "When you said you created the Nexus before, there was so much going on, I didn't realize. The Nexus was formed over two hundred years ago. Are you really that old?" she asked. She noticed the look that went from Grandpappy to Kyra.

"Yes, I am," Kyra replied.

"But how can you still look so young? How long do we live?" asked Betha.

Kyra looked a bit confused, glancing at Grandpappy again. "We live a very long time. I assumed James had spoken to you both about what bonding would do. Did he not?"

Grandpappy rolled his eyes. "You said to keep it simple, Kyra."

Kyra nodded. "We are, but this is pretty basic, old man." She turned back to the young women. "Once you are bonded, your aging slows down. Realistically, you won't die of old age. I'm not sure how old you can get, but you can see I'm not exactly a crone at something over three hundred years." Kyra brushed her hands briskly as though to rid them of that topic. "But interesting facts that aren't particularly relevant to the current situation are not why we are here. We are here so Betha can get some training with opening and closing established portals. Getting you up to speed is critical." The Traveler moved in front of a bright purple door. "Tell me, what do you feel from this door?"

Betha moved up and reached out with her senses. "Wildness, magic, and history." Kyra nodded for her to continue. "It feels friendly."

"It is. This is the doorway to the elven lands. It lands in neutral territory between the two primary fey kingdoms. Try to open the door."

"Is this going to mess with the marketplace outside?" asked Betha.

"No, the portals are down for an hour around now for a break," Kyra said with a smile. "It's the perfect time. Give it a shot."

Betha reached out with a hand, pulling her power and asking for the door to open. She could feel the spark in her hand touch the magic of the door, but nothing happened.

"You need to use a bit more power than that," Kyra said. "Try it again, but this time with a bit more purpose. Tell your power what you want it to do."

Betha reached deeper into her magic and grew the invisible spark in her hand before again touching it to the magic of the door. This time she could feel the connection, but she could also feel the drain on herself. The doorway in front of her went from solid to being made of light. Betha smiled with pride.

"Natural portals are much easier than a tear in the lines," Kyra said.

Betha didn't know how to respond to that, and her confidence faltered. It had been harder than she thought it would be to open this natural portal. Concern radiated through her connection to Angie.

"Was that easy or hard?" asked Kyra.

"It took a bit out of me," answered Betha carefully.

"In the beginning, it can. As you get used to using your power, it gets easier." As Kyra spoke, she opened almost all the doors in the room, causing light to flash in several spots. One doorway remained dark. "You should practice closing the doorways as well. Tears, you would need to treat differently, like trying to stitch together a veil. The veil is what separates our world and others. The goal with tears is not to close them, but to heal them. A tear can happen naturally, but that's pretty uncommon. Travelers of old were tasked with healing natural tears."

"But the Demons are using tears to come here. How many tears are there on Terra?"

Kyra turned away from Betha and studied the archways. "Those aren't natural tears. Something else is causing those."

"Something else? I get that you're not trying to overwhelm me, but this seems important. What else?" Betha looked between Grandpappy and Kyra. "What is letting the demons through?"

Kyra suddenly closed all the portals in the room.

"Someone is cutting through with a knife. It was made from the bones of a Traveler."

"Bones?" whispered Betha. Her mouth opened and closed a few times. She felt Angie's hand on her back.

Kyra continued, "As far as anyone outside of this room is concerned, we don't know how they are doing this. I was trying to ease you into things, but the truth is, we don't have a lot of time. You need to find the knife and destroy it." The older woman looked intently at the two, it was clear she wasn't used to soften such things.

"Wait, me? Why do I need to find it?" asked Betha with some panic.

Kyra tried to look patient and explained. "Because, Betha, I can't leave the Nexus for longer than a few hours. And there isn't anyone else. We are the only Travelers on Terra."

Angie's voice sounded loud in the room. "And without the Nexus, we lose the Accords, and neutrality."

Pride showed in Grandpappy's eyes as he nodded.

"We are the only Travelers?" asked Betha, and her eyebrows drew together.

"Yes. Travelers don't usually stay in one place. I am the exception, since I am holding the Nexus in place," answered Kyra.

"So you actually brought us here not to show us the portals, but to tell us the truth because we are the only ones who can do this," stated Angie in the quiet room.

Kyra nodded, businesslike, but with a touch of sadness in her eyes. "Yes. The Guard is holding back the demons for now, but we will need reinforcements from the Nexus worlds to hold our ground. That will take time, but even then, we can't end it. The more tears you close, the better, but finding the knife is the real goal. Whoever is doing this, once they lose the knife, they can't create any more rifts. This all can't go away until the knife is destroyed."

CHAPTER FIFTEEN

Justin shifted in his seat while the other members of the council trickled into the large auditorium for the meeting. It was a circular room with several ranks of balconies, with all the chairs facing a table in the center. His large frame had never really fit the council seats comfortably, and he'd always had to shift his hips to keep his feet from falling asleep. He brushed his shoulder-length brown hair back from his face as he looked around.

More people than normal had shown up, but given everything that was going on, he didn't blame them. The last ten years on the council had seen some drastic adjustments. When he'd first joined, things were calm, boring even, then changes started happening. First with more manifestations in the human populations, then picking up speed with rarer species making comebacks. Now, tears in the veils with demons coming to Earth, and not to party. Plus, a new Traveler was discovered right under his nose. He was looking forward to hearing what the seer had to say for herself. How did this happen without her knowing?

Finally, the doors closed, and the lights dimmed. The council head took the podium and started the meeting. Justin kept his face neutral, as he always did. The council head was the only human in the room, and he had no idea why the humans had chosen this guy. He always had a sneer and didn't interact much with any of the other members.

"As you are all aware, two more tears have been spotted, along with additional demon attacks. Traveler Kyra has thankfully closed the two that were closest to council lands, but the two newest ones are outside of her effective range. At the moment, the Guard has both additional sites contained. The newest Traveler has progressed in her training and has bonded with an Anchor. We will send teams to the tears to close them shortly. I will now open the floor to questions."

"What are we doing to stop more tears from forming?" The question came from somewhere off to one of the sides of the council hall that Justin could not see. It was a good question, and one that was on everyone's mind.

"We are looking into how these are being created in collaboration with Traveler Kyra and the seer. Unfortunately, progress has been slow, and as yet we have nothing to report, but this is one of our top priorities," answered the council head.

"How long is the draft going to be in effect?" asked a different voice.

Justin flinched at that question and was glad he was

not on the stand. The draft was a drastic measure, but one that he and the other war council members believed was an important step to take. It drafted Others into the Guard to fill the ranks and form additional squads. Given the casualty rates of the Guards holding the tears, it was needed. At the moment, most draftees were still in training. Thankfully, groups of retired Guard had come back into active duty by volunteering.

"As long as necessary to protect our people in this trying time," responded the council head.

"What about the Accords?" another voice from the crowded chamber asked.

"We have reached out to the signatories as required in times of attack, but we all know travel between certain worlds has a time delay, and most of the signatories have their own councils or governments to deal with. We are waiting for responses. It is our fervent hope that our allies, per the terms of the Accords, send help to defend Terra in our time of need, but that help will take time to arrive. We must hold our own until aid comes and a solution to the formation of these tears can be found."

Murmurs picked up across various rows. It was not public knowledge that they were having difficulties getting ahold of the various worlds, and it wouldn't be. They had always known that the time differences would slow down any response from any of the Accord worlds, but the time lag seemed excessive.

"Is the new Traveler still looking for more Anchors?"

Justin's head turned to catch whoever had asked that one, but he couldn't tell. It wasn't a voice he knew. He couldn't believe the question had been asked. As he understood it, becoming an Anchor was a very personal thing. It wasn't like a promotion or something that could be ordered by anyone.

"While it is an honor to be asked to bond, it requires a baseline to start with. The Traveler will bond as they see fit," replied the council head. Justin reflected that for all the man's shortcomings, he was handling some tough questions without being flustered. Maybe the humans hadn't picked so badly after all.

The questions continued, but nothing important came up. Members were concerned about their towns, trade disruption, and the impact of lost Other workforces to the draft—nothing that really mattered in the near term. It dragged on for another hour before the general meeting was dismissed. Justin got up from his chair and headed for the more important meeting of the day, the real reason he was here.

The next meeting room was much smaller and had Guards outside the door. He nodded his head and entered the room. Other members of the war council found their seats. This meeting only held the leaders from each species that had signed the Accords, or their designated representatives. He gave nods to the vampire patron Vincent, Devon from the elves, and Cassandra, head of the witches. Garruk from the trolls and Kellion of the angelic line were in a hushed conversation at the side of the room.

As the door closed, side conversations ended. Everyone took their seats, and Traveler Kyra nodded at the members. The doorway to the room locked, sealing them inside. "I will open the war council with updates.

The first Anchor to be bonded is the shadow wolf." Multiple members turned toward Justin in surprise. Angie was headstrong, and Justin only hoped she could keep Betha safe. While losing her as a long-term Pack member was unfortunate, he was glad that she would now do something she wanted instead of being stuck chasing the whims of the council. Those future battles with her were wiped from the slate, and he was thankful. He would speak to the pup to make sure that Angie would keep an eye on Betha's heart as well. It would be easy for one of the more charming species to play under-handedly.

"How did that happen?" Vincent asked, clearly piqued that the shifters had bonded first.

"It was supposed to happen." Everyone quieted at the seer's voice. Andrea continued, "If it hadn't, then all would have been lost. The demons would have won."

"You are telling us that 'everything' depends on this new Traveler?" probed Vincent.

"This new Traveler is the only one who can close these tears," said Andrea.

Kellion spoke in his deep, resonant voice, "The elves should send help, even the fey. They have casters who can close tears."

"The elves *are* sending help. The fey are at war, and we only have maybe a ten percent chance that we will receive help from them in time." Andrea's voice held a note of finality that even Kellion would not argue with. Justin's eyes flickered over to Devon, who nodded.

The room turned to silence at that. Most had been counting on the fey warriors to help with the demons.

Andrea continued, "And before you ask, Kellion has already sent word to the angels, but as you know, I can't see into that world. The time difference there is worse than with the fey. We have at least another week before a response would even be possible."

Several people in the room glanced at Kellion—the tall, dark-haired, blue-eyed angel—but his face was blank.

"So you really are saying the new Traveler is the only hope of closing these tears for good?" asked Vincent.

Kyra moved to speak. "She is young but strong. She will do what needs to be done, but she will need a team of the best to support her. At her age, one Anchor will not cut it, but she isn't one to take on Anchors just to get stronger. In the long run, that is a good thing, but given our situation, it adds to the danger. Whoever is on that team needs to know, no matter what, she needs to live. There is also the increased chance that whoever is on that team will become an Anchor. So that's the good with the bad."

Justin wondered how many around the table would now search their family trees for someone suitable. He had to give Kyra credit. She knew what to say to a bunch of powerful creatures. Several members of the war council would do almost anything to have a Traveler in their pocket, including playing dirty.

CHAPTER SIXTEEN

The footsteps coming her way weren't a concern, or at least Betha didn't think they were. She caught the scent, and it was very pine and musky. Then the smell of wet dog came to her nose. A smile came over her face and she looked up from the picnic table. The weather was basically showing off, with sunshine, blue skies, and the perfect temperature. Ben and Joey headed toward her table. She gave them a little wave and went back to studying. She was getting better at using the senses that had come from bonding with Angie. It was still fresh enough that if she wasn't thinking, they didn't work. But if she focused, she understood what all the showers had been for.

Seeing Joey reminded her that she needed to see if maybe he would like to play ball again. It fulfilled her childhood wish of getting a dog, but at the same time, she didn't know how the rest of the Pack would react. He had enjoyed the last time they had played, so maybe it wasn't taboo. Or maybe Angie wanted to play ball with

Joey. No one was ever playing in the courtyard in shifter shape.

The two guys took seats at the table, setting down their own books. "You snagged the best table on campus." Ben's statement was correct, since it had an umbrella and was near the coffeehouse so she could people-watch as well as study.

Looking up, Betha said, "I got here before the line at the coffeehouse formed for breakfast sandwiches. Today is a no-training day, so I need to get caught up on homework."

Joey peered at the books and assignments on the table. "At least this is the easier work. I remember doing some of this in high school."

Betha tried not to let her emotions show on her face. She was struggling with the catch-up work. They both must have caught wind of her frustration since Joey amended quickly, "Whoa, I didn't mean it like that—just that if you need help, I might get to sound smart."

Betha couldn't help it, and she reached over to ruffle his hair. "You are smart." Joey seemed to be more like his old self, and it was so good to see.

"You shouldn't spoil him," Ben chimed in. "But if you need help, all you need to do is ask."

Betha nodded. "I know, but a part of me feels that some of this is worthless. Way more important things are happening in the world right now."

"The basics are important. Plus, all that Demon stuff they have you reading is not basic."

"Thanks, Angie." Betha was still getting used to random messages from Angie. The connection wasn't as

blurry, which was good, but it still shocked her to get a response to her feelings. Angie could listen in much better to her than she could to Angie. She really didn't mind, though sometimes it did get a little frustrating. Angie assured her that it would even out over time, but for now, it felt a little like her best friend was always looking over her shoulder.

"What are you guys working on today?" asked Betha.

Joey rolled his eyes and motioned to his laptop. "The demon reading and assignment. Supposed to write a paper on how I would use my strengths to fight a demon. I don't really want to touch that with a ten-foot pole. Been there, done that, didn't go so well."

Ben nodded. "Totally with Joey on this one. I wrote up a summary of what I did at the nightclub fight, which I figured was good enough. I need to get ahead in math. It's one of the few courses that didn't change with the draft. Other than that, my programming courses are so easy I can do them in my sleep."

Betha cocked her head to the side. "You were drafted?"

"Yeah, I got my notice a few days ago. Since our Pack requires basic training, I still have time to try to finish up my studies for the semester. It helps that basic training is on campus since it doubles as one facility. Did you get a notice?"

Betha shook her head. "No, I am on a modified schedule since I manifested so late. I'm already working with Carter most days."

"Ask them if they want snacks. I'm almost at the front of the line," sent Angie.

"Oh, do you guys want something from the coffeehouse? Angie is almost at the counter."

Joey looked confused, but he rattled off a list. Ben just added some drinks to Joey's order.

"You can really talk with her?" asked Joey once Ben was done.

"Yeah, she says it is like the Pack link, but not," Betha shrugged. "It is what it is. I wouldn't change it."

Her homework sounded like a better and better idea. Better than the topic of her and Angie. Instead, though, she asked, "What about you, Joey? Did you get drafted?" Everything inside her really hoped that he hadn't.

"Yeah, I got a notice—I am still faster and stronger than a human, but I'll be staying in this form."

Betha didn't even realize she had reached out for his hand.

"Uh, guys, hand here!" Ben and Joey darted to their feet to help Angie, who was carrying two drink carriers and a few bags of goodies. "I got all the things, I think, so we should be able to get the homework done."

They passed food and drinks around the table, including a large amount in front of Betha. "I can't believe I can eat this much."

"You need to if you want to add more muscle. I am surprised you have been able to add the definition you got already..." Ben's voice trailed off as everyone at the table looked at him. He immediately turned bright red. "Not that I am studying your assets, but it is noticeable." His face was turning redder and redder as he spoke, but he kept on digging. "I mean, I am assuming it has to do with bonding with Angie. Your strength has increased, along with your scent and power level."

"That is observant of you," said Angie in a deadpan voice. It broke the silence that followed. Even Joey was looking at Ben like he'd lost it.

"I think Ben likes you," sent Angie. Betha ignored the comment since he wasn't the one she fantasized about. Her blue-eyed trainer had caught her eye from day one and hadn't left her head since. Betha was pretty sure Angie knew it too.

Joey tried to save the day by jumping back into the conversation. "Angie, did you get a notice?"

She nodded. "I did, but they revoked it after we bonded. Anchors aren't subject to the draft. Our priority is to our Traveler. If something happened to us, it would weaken them too much. I have some extra training I'm doing though."

"I didn't know that. Who are you training with?" asked Betha. She couldn't believe Angie was fitting additional training in somewhere. Then again, Betha wasn't sure how many classes Angie was really going to anymore. Or what homework she would still have.

"Grandpappy is training me," said Angie before she took a long sip of her iced coffee. Betha realized Angie was trying to avoid eye contact with Joey.

Joey bumbled on, unaware. "Does that mean you are free from all the rules that Justin had for you?"

Now Betha was invested, and she wished she had popcorn. Instead, she pulled a brownie out of the bag that Angie had set on the table. Ben gave her a smile and nodded his head toward Joey. Betha wished she knew what he was trying to say. It was true Angie was not free from the dating restrictions that Justin has placed on Angie.

"It seems to be that way," said Angie hesitantly.

"Does that mean you will join Betha and me at our weekly session of fetch?" asked Joey.

Ben looked like he was going to die, and Betha did her best not to laugh. Of all the questions he could have asked, that was the one. Joey was Joey. Also, when did fetch become a weekly occurrence. They had played once.

"Fetch?" asked Angie. It was clear that was not what she expected to be asked.

"Yeah, it'll be great! We can run together!"

The train wreck was, fortunately, stopped as someone approached the table.

"Hey Betha! I heard you are a Traveler—that's so cool!" commented Susan as she came up to the group. Betha knew her from her first day and her economics class. "I stopped by your room, but it was empty."

Betha was glad for the interruption. She could feel a mess of emotions from Angie, but she couldn't really suss out what they meant. "They moved my dorm to a different area of campus, something to do with safety. Thanks for encouraging me to get my arm checked out at the health center. It kinda started this whole thing. Oh, do you remember Angie, Ben, and Joey?" Betha motioned around the table as they exchanged hellos. Betha caught the exchange of interest between Susan and Joey.

A flash of anger came from Angie as Joey made eyes

at Susan. Betha put her hand on Angie's arm, but the anger wasn't visible on her friend at all.

"Nice to run into all of you again. Betha, wanna exchange numbers and we can catch up later?"

"Sure!" Betha gave out her number and noticed that both Ben and Joey added it to their phones as well.

"We should catch up soon!" Susan did a small wave and then headed to the coffee shop.

Betha noticed Joey was watching the attractive woman walk away with a distinct look of interest. "Is she your type, my friend?" Betha asked as she elbowed him. Angie went still on the other side of her.

"Well, I mean, she is pretty, most of the angelic are. But she wouldn't run with me under the moonlight or play ball." He shrugged. "It wouldn't be serious either way. I have my sights set on someone, but they are way out of my league."

Betha was surprised that Joey seemed a bit of a realist when it came to women. "Aw, you would be a catch for any shifter."

Joey gave Betha a small smile, but it seemed fake. "Thanks, I hope so. Maybe someday it will work out." He seemed to avoid looking at Angie.

"So, do I know this special someone?" asked Betha.

Now it was Joey's turn to blush. "Well, let's not talk about it. I don't want to jinx my chances. Plus homework, right? Homework."

"Do you play ball, Ben?" asked Betha, giving Joey a break.

"Ball?" Ben blinked at the question, looking up from his notes.

"Yeah, like with a tennis ball. Though I guess maybe a beach ball would work—you could boop it with your nose." The smile in her voice matched a twinkle in Angie's eyes.

"I haven't. You know what would be better?" asked Ben. "We could play beach volleyball at the sandpit this evening. Might be a fairer game, and we'd all get to stay human-shaped."

Everyone started discussing the idea of beach volleyball, and who would be on whose team, but it remained undecided. They were all clearly trying to avoid doing their homework, but that was hardly a surprise.

A wave of satisfaction came over Betha. This was what she had been hoping for when she came here, to this school. The feelings of friends and belonging. Now she needed to get Angie to go out with Joey, and all would be right with the world. If you ignored the demons.

~

CARTER DID NOT WANT to make this phone call, yet there wasn't anyone he trusted more. He could always count on his brother, even though he didn't always agree with his choices. Finally, he pressed call and waited.

"Hey Carter, what's up? Wanna finally take a vacation and check out this beach with me?" asked Eric.

Carter resisted rolling his eyes. "I take it you haven't been kept in the loop on your little adventure?"

"What loop? I am in the sun relaxing, flirting with the beach girls. You know how they all go for me."

"The loop where tears from the hells are opening and demons are invading Terra?" asked Carter. The silence on the line was unexpected.

"You are joking, right?"

Carter pulled the phone away and looked at it in disbelief. "No, didn't Kellion loop you in?" The truly eloquent and creative swearing on the other end of the line answered that question. He had no idea how someone could be so far out of the loop that they didn't know that this was going on. Then again, this was Eric.

"No, he introduced me to this chick he was hoping I would click with a few weeks ago. Are demons really invading?"

"Yeah, and I need your help for a team I am on."

"Oh, so you need your big brother's help, do you?"

And this was why he hadn't wanted to make the call. "I trust you, and I need you to join my team." He needed someone he trusted. The council was important, but he had seen the drama that had happened when Angie had been discovered as a shadow wolf. Carter knew the longer-lived races on the council had more experience than he had, but assassins were not the way. He was thankful that option was off of the table. They didn't need to get their claws into Betha, who wasn't even under their rule. He hoped his twin would see things his way.

"Dude, you know I'll be happy to come lead this little team of yours. What's a few demons, anyway?" Eric replied, and the line went dead.

Carter sighed, hoping he'd done the right thing.

CHAPTER SEVENTEEN

Homework was done, and everyone had gone their separate ways to drop off their stuff. Betha was heading back from her new dorm room toward the trailhead that led to the volleyball courts when she heard someone jogging behind her. A quick glance over her shoulder caused a smile to come across her face.

"I am shocked to not see Angie nearby," said Carter as he slowed down. He was wearing workout shorts and no shirt. He looked like he had been running for some time. Betha tried hard not to stare, but he looked downright gorgeous. "You sure you should be out wandering alone?"

"Let me enjoy the moment," answered Betha before blushing. "I had to argue with Angie to be able to go to my room and back without supervision. Don't worry, I am meeting folks at the trailhead. We all decided on some volleyball down at the sandpit. It's glorious weather for it."

Carter nodded. Betha noticed that he didn't pick up his pace, keeping beside her instead.

"Let me guess, you are jogging in that direction?" said Betha.

He flashed her a smile. "Maybe. We are having some fantastic weather." Carter received an eye roll for that comment. It seemed like she had an escort to the trailhead, whether or not she wanted one. She didn't mind though, despite her slight embarrassment at him escorting her. Her friends came into view, and Carter picked up his speed.

"Enjoy volleyball!" He called out over his shoulder as he passed her on the left and kept going down the path. Betha's eyes tracked him as he went—she couldn't help herself.

"You're drooling," sent Angie.

Betha quickly caught up to her friends. "Carter didn't want me walking alone," said Betha as she approached.

"Did you see his abs? How does he do that?" asked Joey. "Like, I know he is human, but, like, are we sure? You thought Betha was." He turned toward Angie, who was just shaking her head.

"I do not know how he stays in shape the way he does," said Angie.

Ben chimed in. "Abs are all about diet. He must eat clean and put in the work. It's his job to keep up with us shifters. I would be more shocked if he wasn't in shape and could still keep up."

Betha could not believe the conversation and tried to keep the image of Carter out of her head. All she needed was her friends to pick up on how she felt about him.

Well, the friends other than Angie. She couldn't hide it from Angie.

"So you are saying, if I ate better, I could have defined abs like that?" asked Joey.

Ben nodded. "I bet you could even ask Carter for help, and you would have them much quicker than a human."

Angie glanced at Betha and changed the subject. "I claim Betha on my team for volleyball!"

Joey stopped walking. "Not fair. You guys have that head thing. How about it's me and you versus Ben and Betha? The two B's versus us?"

"I think that is a great idea," said Betha before Angie could complain.

"Really, Betha?"

Betha gave Angie a giant grin. This was going to be great. The courts were just up ahead once the trees ended. But then her chest felt warm, and her mark felt weird. Her pace picked up as something drew her toward the courts.

"Whoa, Betha, you good?" asked Angie.

"Yeah, just want to make sure we get a court," Betha responded distractedly.

"Liar." Angie's voice caused the guys to pick up the pace as well.

"Something feels weird. We need to move faster," commented Betha. She broke out into a run. The trail took a turn, and ahead she could see someone in the trees, wearing a hoodie. Her mark flared, and she watched as the person stabbed the air with a knife. The knife vanished, and all Betha could see was their hand. Strange light flickered in the air. They had used a knife!

"Portal!" Betha yelled. She darted forward as Angie fumbled with her phone. They both had an emergency alert button to give a warning. Sirens started blaring over campus.

"Joey, watch Betha!" yelled Angie, tossing the phone his way.

The knife in the person's hand stopped in midair, and they pulled it down. Strange light flickered from the knife, like the stranger was drawing in the air. Betha's heart pounded, and she could feel the tearing as if it were her chest being cut into. Pain washed over her, but she forced herself forward. The knife called to her. Only sixty more feet. Out of the corner of her eye, she watched a shadow dart to the tree line.

A roar from behind her let her know Ben had changed into his bear form, and the sound of his feet hitting the ground told her he was charging. This would not be the nightclub—they could stop this!

The figure was fast and completed the vertical stroke. With the first cut done, they moved faster, cutting a line across the first. The pain inside her turned into something else. Betha didn't understand it, but she didn't think the pain was hers. It was almost as if the leyline itself was crying.

Angie in wolf form hit the figure, knocking them away from the tear.

"Get the knife!" echoed in Betha's head.

Something reached out of the portal, and its talons

pulled at the edges of the flickering light. It was one of those things from the nightclub—a dog demon. Betha kept running full speed toward the tear, hoping that it wouldn't get through. The tear widened from a line to a gaping hole, and the creature pulled itself onto the ground. Then it screamed. Betha almost tripped over her own feet trying to stop. She couldn't fight that; she didn't even have a weapon on her. She had to get around it to the tear.

"Shit!" Betha didn't know what to do.

An answering growl came from Ben—a black bear larger than even Angie in her wolf form—as he ran past Betha. He tackled the creature. Betha swore the ground shook as he hit the demon. Once the horrible thing focused on Ben, she sped back up, keeping her eyes on the tear. Only ten more feet. The creature had widened it, and Betha could see through it to a different world on the other side. It led to the inside of what looked to be a cavern with flickering torches. More of those creatures were running toward the open portal. They were like a pack of Dobermans with giant heads, talons, fangs, and spikes running down their spines. The one leading the rest of the pack locked eyes with her. The bright red eyes stared at her, its tongue lolling between its fangs with drool flying out of its mouth. Betha gathered her power, touching the end of the tear, forcing herself not to flee in terror.

"Please heal." The warmth from her hand became an inferno. It flared bright white and was completely visible, streaming from her palm to the tear itself, which glowed brightly in response. Her eyes were still on the creature, which jumped toward her. It was going to make it through the portal. The tear was closing, but she could see the claws stretched out. The outline of the tear turned silver with the same light as her power. It spread from the edges to the center. The portal was closing, and Betha could feel relief from somewhere.

Even though the claws were faster, Betha didn't dare move. Pain lanced through her side. She did not stop. The demon tried to pull her through to the other side, but she dug her feet in. "No, you will not! I will close it!" It hurt; she didn't know something could hurt like this. Then she toppled backward as the tear finally closed, slicing the creature's claws off. Her stomach hurt, and she could smell her own blood, but it was done. "You're welcome," she whispered, not knowing who or what she was talking to. The pain inside her chest was gone, replaced by searing pain in her stomach.

The sky was very blue, and Betha wondered if they were going to get to play volleyball, and if her team would win. Angie was above her, frantically calling out to someone, but Betha couldn't understand what she was saying. Darkness started to take over, and she struggled to touch Angie.

"We got you. It's okay," Angie said.

Betha tried to look around for the others and saw Carter running toward them. She started to smile, then everything went black.

CHAPTER EIGHTEEN

Angie was trying her best not to pace back and forth in the hallway of the medical center on campus. The fucker who had opened the portal got away. He was fast, but Angie was faster. She almost had him, tearing his hoodie and catching a glance of his demonic eyes. Then she had felt Betha get stabbed with claws. That distraction was all he needed to get away from her. She and Betha needed to work on the distraction through the link. It had come up in passing, but now they really had to figure it out; the feeling of claws digging into Betha had stopped Angie cold. It took too long to realize it was Betha who was hurt, not her.

Now Betha was recovering, but Joey was not. Sweet Joey had gone after the demon who got around Angie. He was now with a healer, and they were trying to save his foot. Ben had taken out the demon that had gotten through the portal, giving Betha time to close the portal, which was his job. They had saved the day, but it didn't feel like it.

"I can feel your frustration from here. You need to tell Joey how you feel."

Angie's eyes widened in shock, and she dashed into Betha's room. The room smelled of whatever the healer had put on Betha's stomach. It was herbal and made her want to lick her best friend. At least it didn't smell like disinfectant.

"You're awake," said Angie.

Betha could barely keep her eyes open. "Yeah, totally need to sleep some more, but I could hear you all the way in here."

Angie ran a hand over her face. "Ugh, I'm sorry. I'll try to keep it down." She had been pacing in the hallway —despite her best effort—back and forth between Betha's room and Joey's room. At least the healers and doctors hadn't asked her to leave.

"What's going on with Joey? Why are you so worried?" asked Betha.

"He might lose his foot. It was completely shattered, and now it's healing wrong. If I had only been faster." Angie froze when that last part slipped out.

"It is not your fault. A demon opened a portal on campus, and he is to blame. Not you. It is his fault this whole thing is happening. Otherwise, we would be in class, talking about parties and figuring out where we wanted to intern. So, not your fault," said Betha. Her eyes started to slip closed. *"You need to tell him you like him, though,"*

"You need some sleep, Betha. I'll go see if there is an update on his condition." Angie gave her hand a squeeze. She prayed Betha would look less pale the next time she awoke. The healer had closed her wounds and wasn't concerned. She had said it was mostly from Betha using so much power at once, without more training, that she had passed out.

Angie shook her head, moving into the hallway. As she made her way to where Joey was, she caught Ben's scent. He was standing outside the room with a frown. His head jerked to her. His voice was more of a growl than normal as he said, "You need to talk some sense into him. The healers say he needs to lose the foot and that there is only a slight chance that he will recover. Otherwise, he will be in constant pain. He doesn't want to do it. Thinks without the foot he won't ever be anything but a cripple." Angie realized tears were rolling down her cheeks only when Ben pulled her into a big hug. "Shh...it's okay. I didn't mean to dump this on you. I know you and Joey are close."

It took longer than she wanted, but she calmed down. "I'll speak to him," she finally said, sniffling. It was hard pulling herself out of Ben's hug. He had always been like a brother to her. Now Joey—he was complicated. She realized what her Grandpappy had meant when he said that the road she had chosen would be a hard one.

Angie knocked lightly on the door and entered. Her eyes darted around, landing on Joey. His leg was elevated, and she could smell the pain and worry in the room. Joey turned to look at her and tried to smile.

"Joey, boy," whispered Angie.

Tears rolled down his face, and she moved forward. She leaned over him, thankful that the bed was high as she pulled him to her chest. His tears soaked her shirt, and she patted his back. “It will be okay. You’ll see.”

“I might not run again,” Joey sobbed. “They want to take my foot. who is going to want me with one foot?” His voice was muffled, but Angie could hear him. She didn’t stop holding him close.

“I will always be here.” She squeezed him tight but was worried about hitting his foot with the awkward position. Angie kissed the top of his head. “You will always be my Joey, no matter what.”

He pulled away slightly. “You can’t mean that.” He looked at her with utter confusion. “I am me, and you are a shadow wolf.”

“You are you, and you are my Joey.” She moved in and kissed him lightly on the lips, though he didn’t respond. As she pulled away, his confusion was still there, but now mixed with hope. “I don’t care what other people think; that doesn’t stop how I feel.”

A knock sounded at the door, and Angie pulled away. She hadn’t been paying attention to her surroundings. Carter walked in, followed by someone who looked really similar to him, but maybe younger. “Carter?” asked Angie.

“Oh, Angie, I didn’t know you would be here. My brother arrived, and I am hoping he can help with Joey’s foot. Eric, meet Angie and Joey,” Carter said, indicating each in turn.

“Nice to meet you two,” Eric said in a rich voice. He moved around the bed toward Joey’s foot. “I have some healing abilities, and I might be able to go a step further than the healer here.”

"What do you mean, further?" asked Joey.

Angie realized Eric was a Nephilim, with his perfect skin and blond hair. They always seemed to have a pull, and once you understood what it was, it was easy to spot those with angelic blood. It must be where he got his healing ability. Half-angels often had powers that were different from the more common abilities.

"I am hoping to save your foot," continued Eric, "but I need permission to get started. I can't make any promises, but I will try. You did a good thing protecting the young Traveler. Twice now. That deserves the best I have to offer."

Joey looked toward Carter, who nodded his head in confirmation. It was his brother, after all, and Carter was trustworthy. "I mean, might as well try," he said.

Eric nodded and unwrapped the bandages. "Angie, you should leave—this will not be pleasant." Her eyes went back to Carter, and she could tell he wanted to speak to her. She turned to look at Joey, who looked starstruck and hopeful.

"I'll check in on you later. Get some rest, and remember—no matter what." Angie kissed his forehead and headed out the door before he could reply. Carter followed, closed the door, and motioned her down the hall. Ben was nowhere to be seen. "Your brother randomly shows up when Joey needs to be healed?" she asked him.

Carter rolled his eyes. She never thought that would happen—he was always deep in trainer mode. "You know better than that. Given the attack on campus, the council is putting together a team for Betha. Kellion recommended Eric since he can heal and has some angel fire. It will help with the demons." Things always went to business quickly with Carter.

"Who else is on this team?" asked Angie.

"So far, me and Eric. No one else has met my requirements."

"Betha should be in on these conversations," Angie argued.

"The council does what it wants, and given that she didn't even know she was a Traveler, she doesn't get much say. Eric will be an excellent addition—he has training. Plus his abilities will be useful. I would be more worried about who else is going to show up. I trust my twin, but I don't trust whomever the council wants to get involved. As of now, you should be Betha's shadow. You guys did well with sounding the alarm and closing the portal. That could have been much worse than it was. We are counting this as a win."

"He got away, though," muttered Angie.

"Yeah, but you and Joey injured him. It should buy us time to get some tears closed. Right now, we need all the time we can get."

Angie narrowed her eyes. "Tears? As in, plural, and open?"

Carter shrugged. "Need-to-know basis, Angie. They are keeping everything locked down so people don't panic. Including Betha."

"Are they pushing Eric to become an Anchor?"

Carter's eyes closed for a moment, and he took a breath. "I am assuming so. I am sticking nearby to make sure nothing happens without Betha's consent. Eric is pretty, powerful, and charming as heck. He is very full of himself, and he will put pressure on Betha. To him, this is another status symbol. While I don't doubt you two could handle it, I will feel better being nearby. Plus, as you know, I'm a pretty good shot."

Angie chuckled. He was better than that—he was an excellent shot. He held several records, beating out Others of several types. In many ways, he was an example of the best physical achievement humans had to offer. For now though, they needed to concentrate on getting back on their feet. Plus, now it sounded like there were going to be some changes, and that meant more work to do. Not to mention the demon opening these tears now knew a Traveler was on campus. Once Betha was back up, Angie would mention that she was moving in. She meant to take Carter's suggestion very seriously indeed.

~

THE DEMON MOVED SLOWLY down the street. He stuck to the shadows and alleyways to cover his scent. Anger rolled off of him in waves as he headed to a basement door. He made his way inside, slamming the door behind him.

"Sir! What happened to you?" A butler darted forward and pulled out a chair. "They hurt you! We should go back to our world and get this treated!"

"I am not going back to be jumped and have my title taken from me. Bandage this up and bring me a slave so I can heal." The demon sat in the chair and removed his hood. He looked almost human, but his eyes gave him away. They were red and blue, matching the symbols glowing beneath his skin. "They have a new Traveler. She closed the portal before I could let chaos reign on the campus."

"I warned you about Pack lands. They have many shifters about! We need to tell the king about the Traveler. This could change his plans on Caledonia."

The demon grabbed the butler's shirt. "You aren't telling my father anything until I bring that Traveler to him. I want to know everything about that girl. She is my key. Father would do anything for a Traveler under his control."

"This is beyond what we were told," the butler complained weakly. "As is, the king knows nothing of this. That's dangerous, sire!"

The prince growled, "Plans change. We are going to get that girl and cement my place as heir to the throne. My sister won't even see it coming." A dark smile covered his face, showing pointed fangs protruding slightly past the rest of his pointed teeth. "Go get that slave. I need to heal."

The butler left, and the prince tried to relax back in the chair. His leg throbbed, but the pain didn't bother him. Just another flesh wound that would heal with the right type of snack. His mind raced as he tried to figure out his next steps. This wonderful opportunity wouldn't have fallen in his lap if his sister hadn't been named heir. Maybe that wasn't the disaster he'd thought it was. With care, this could be the biggest opportunity of his life.

THE BUTLER MADE his way out of the room and kept his face clear until he reached the hallway. Then he shook his head and scowled. The prince was going to get in trouble for this from the king. The only reason he had shown the prince how to wield the knife was so that he would stop trying to cause wars at home. The butler was a loyal servant of the king and of the king's household. Ever since the princess royal had been named heir, things had gotten out of control. With the king away and the princess royal acting as regent, there was no one to control the prince. This was a mess, and he had accidentally started it, even though he had been trying to help.

Somehow, he needed to get out of this alive, and he wasn't at all sure how he was going to do it. A thought occurred to him, slowly dawning as he dragged a slave out of the pens to take to the angry prince. *I need to survive, but maybe the prince doesn't, since his sister was named heir. Maybe I can find a way to fix all of this without losing my head in the process.*

CHAPTER NINETEEN

The mood in the SUV was dark, dreary, and depressed, reflecting the rain and clouds outside. Betha sat in the back with Eric while Carter drove and Angie rode shotgun. Eric kept trying to start a conversation with Betha, but everything was grim. It felt like she was being directed on everything that she should be doing, not allowed to make independent choices, not trusted to run her own life.

It had been a week since she had closed the tear on campus, and that week had been spent training with Carter and Eric. Joey was doing okay. Eric was able to save his foot, but he still wasn't walking. The council had kept the fact that there were two open tears being managed by the Guard from her the whole time. And that demons would sporadically come through those tears, and Guard members were dying. Betha was frustrated that the council hid how many tears were open and how many people had died.

Part of her understood why. She had been knocked

down hard by closing that tear on campus. The other part of her just grew angrier and more bitter every time she thought about it. Wherever they were driving, her frustration made her want to growl like Angie did. The closer they got, the more it felt like someone was touching the center of her shoulder blades with a needle. It wasn't painful, but it was like she could feel it was causing pain to someone else. The forest surrounding the roads seemed never-ending, and it fit her mood. This was the deepest into Pack lands she had ever been. From what she could tell, it was all native forest, untouched by humans or Others in centuries.

"At least they weren't going to toss you at a problem without a chance to survive it." Angie's voice in her head caused her frown to deepen.

"I know, it just feels like a betrayal." Betha hadn't been able to hide how she felt about Carter from Angie. While she knew Carter hadn't betrayed her, it still sucked.

"I know you two are probably having a grand old conversation, but want to let us in on it?" asked Eric. Betha wasn't sure why Eric had been added to the team. Every time he opened his mouth, she had an urge to punch him. His too-good-looks, cocky attitude, tendency to talk down to everyone— including his own brother— and just slightly inauthentic charm all grated on her. But mostly, it was just another choice about her life that had been made without her. Maybe she didn't have a right to resent him for choices he hadn't made, but Betha was reveling in that resentment anyway.

"We were just discussing how someone should have let me know there were two tears just doing their thing, disgorging demons and killing people." Betha couldn't believe how whiny her voice sounded.

Carter turned the car down a gravel road, and Betha caught his eye in the mirror. He stared at her for a moment before answering. "I was only looped in last week once the fighting had lessened. Before then there was no way to even get you close to it. Now we have heavy guns set up and a clear way to approach. Before this, it was almost a never-ending wave. We are still trying to get the second one under control. Thankfully, they are away from civilization and the Guard are the only ones around. The Guard is stretched thin, and closing this one would give them—well, us—a break." Carter took a deep breath. "Betha, it isn't going to be pretty once we get out of this car. We are approaching a literal battlefield."

Eric made a wave. "Don't scare her, Carter. This should be a walk in the park. A little angel fire and I can take care of the demons."

"I don't like how he is dismissing Carter," thought Angie toward Betha.

"Same, Angie, same."

"Do you feel anything as we get closer?" asked Angie out loud.

"It is less like getting stabbed, like the one on campus was, and more like an open wound. And yes, it's getting stronger."

The sound of heavy artillery shook the car, and the talking stopped. Trees on either side of the road were hacked off, creating distance between the rest of the forest and the road. Concrete roadblocks formed a funnel and created a checkpoint with Guards on either side. Carter drove through it with a wave and parked the car near a tent. "Let's do this," he said, almost to himself.

Up until now, she had done really well avoiding thinking about what was going to happen once she got out of the SUV. Carter was the first to get out, followed by Eric. Some guys in uniform began to chat with them. Angie got out of the SUV and took a moment to look over things before she motioned Betha out of the car.

Betha took a look around to get her bearings. The ground was muddy gravel, and piles of trees formed a wall in the distance. This had to all have been forest before the tear had opened. Canvas tents were set up, but she wasn't tall enough to see anything else.

The two soldiers saluted Carter and grabbed the bags out of the back. "We have a tent for you to gear up," said the taller of the two.

"What's the status?" asked Carter.

"There was a surge this morning at both sites, but we have it under control here. We purposely let them gain ground at Site C, and it has reduced the amount of demon activity here."

Betha followed Carter into the tent with Angie taking the rear. Fear and uncertainty churned inside her. The spot behind her shoulder blades seemed to shift.

"We've got this Betha, don't worry," commented Angie quietly.

Eric pulled the gear out of the duffle bags and motioned for Betha to get started. She had armor to wear and had spent last week getting used to it. Her weapons were a small caliber handgun, along with a short sword.

Having a weapon at all was a last resort, mostly so she felt like she could protect herself rather than for her to actually use them. While she could shoot reasonably well, she hadn't been tested under pressure. The short sword was much less familiar, but she figured if things got really bad, she'd just remember to stick them with the pointy end.

The armor went on first, and Angie kept guard at the door. The two Guards that were there looked a bit insulted, but Betha knew it didn't faze Angie at all.

Once Betha was done and Eric had donned his own armor, Angie changed. She quickly stripped facing a tent wall. One moment she was human, then a giant black wolf was there. Betha smiled at her friend and couldn't help but scratch her ears. Angie's head was almost to Betha's chest. She was terrifying, but not to Betha. The wolf breath, on the other hand, was still horrible.

Carter looked over the group and nodded. He started attaching weapons to his own armor hardpoints. "Everyone knows the plan. If shit hits the fan, Angie gets Betha back here." A look passed between the human and the wolf.

"You might want to prepare yourself. There is a crowd outside the tent," sent Angie.

"A crowd?" asked Betha out loud.

"Yeah, lots of scents."

"Traveler Betha." Betha looked up from Angie to the officer who had spoken. "My men are outside and ready to go. They will do what it takes to get you to that portal."

Betha nodded. "You just have to get me there, and I

will get it closed. If they see me coming, they might surge." She had no idea if the mysterious demon with the knife had spread the word on what she looked like.

"We are prepared for that," he replied. She knew that meant that they were prepared to die, if necessary.

Carter took the lead, heading out the door with resolve, and she followed. Angie stayed by her side, and Eric took the rear. She tried to prepare herself for the eyes, but they all reached out to her. She didn't understand why they were looking at her like that.

"You are giving them hope."

The word "hope" punched her in the stomach, and she gritted her teeth. Betha did her best to keep her emotions from her face. She had heard this group would be a mixed Guard, and she had been confused. Seeing them, she understood. Several were in shifted forms, and she could see elves along with trolls. All looked ready for battle.

"Guard! Form up!" The Guard moved around them, covering their front and sides. The wall of fallen trees was closer than she'd thought. It blocked her view of the actual battleground. She could feel the pulse of the tear in front of her. It was a distance away, and that worried her. How much of no-man's-land did they need to cross?

The ground shook as the giant guns began to fire. The group of Guard charged, but Carter held their team back. Then, without any signal Betha could see, the four of them were moving forward. Carter kept them as far away from the screaming and gunfire as possible. They were not approaching the tear head-on. They moved following the wall, keeping it between them and the tear. She knew it was part of the plan, but all of the Guard members were charging straight in toward a gap in the wall. The realization that those Guard members were bait—not much more than a distraction—hit her at the same time she felt something happening to the tear.

"More of them are coming through." Her voice was soft, but Carter held up a hand to stop them from moving. He whispered something into his coms. The feeling vanished, and Betha relayed the info. The wall wasn't towering overhead as much, and she could see where it stopped.

Carter spoke into his mic and then nodded to the group. "Now is our chance! Nothing is near the edges of the battlefield, and the demons that are here are going after the Guard."

Then they were running. The wall ended, and now it was forest on the left. On the right were some trees but mostly hills, boulders, and underbrush. Thank the fates she had been running every day with her gear. Her training had prepared her for this part, at least. It didn't prepare her for Carter shooting things that came at them, or all of the blood. Eric had his sword out and used it as demon dogs got close. Angie kept herself in between the demons and Betha. The tear was close—she could feel the echo of pain—and she kept running.

"I am coming. I am almost there," she whispered to that pain. It seemed to pause in her mind, which was strange. They had cleared the trees, and Betha could finally see what was going on. In that moment, she froze. It was horrible. Hordes of demonic creatures used talons and fangs to attack the Guard, who were giving at least as good as they got, but dying all the same.

Betha focused on the tear. Her gaze moved to where that presence was in her mind. It was a giant tear, much larger than the one on campus. From where she was, she could see that other world again, only this time it wasn't a cavern. Instead, burned trees, smoky skies, and rubble littered her view. Fires burned somewhere off in the distance, and as the smoke moved, she realized the ground was covered with bones. Each time the smoke drifted in the wind, it uncovered more—piles and piles of bones. Yet nothing else moved. At the moment, there weren't any demons on the other side.

"We need to move," Carter whispered. They started running again, this time with Betha leading the way. She could feel where she needed to start.

She let go of the gun as they approached the tear, letting it drop from her fingers as she began to gather her power. As she reached out to the edge of the tear, that pain came again, and she flinched. It then lessened as she started to feed her power into the tear. "You need to heal and close. I will help you; you will be healed," she whispered as she worked.

The warmth spread along the wavy lines floating in midair, and the outside edges of the tear turned silver, becoming more visible in the light. Howls sounded behind them, but Betha focused on the tear.

"We got this Betha. Just close that thing."

Gunshots sounded behind her, but she didn't dare turn around. The tear had started as wide as a school bus, but the bright silver light twisted and writhed, and the opening shrank. Now it was closer to the size of a car. The farthest edge moved nearer to her as the tear continued to shrink. The pain inside her head lessened, but the sounds of fighting were coming closer.

Faith in her friends filled her. Faith that they could do this. Even Eric, despite her distaste. Her breathing had gotten worse, and her chest felt tight, but they were so close. "I need you to close, to heal." A flash of warmth came from the tear, and it snapped closed. Betha fell forward on one of her knees, but remained upright, to her own surprise.

"We did it," she whispered, about ready to collapse.

"Betha, move!" shouted Carter.

Angie butted her out of the way, and Betha realized that the demons on this side were now pinned between them and the rest of the Guard. She reached back, grabbing her gun from the ground where it had fallen, but when she looked up, she froze. Eric's sword was covered in white flame, and it sliced through every demon it touched. Angie took out anything that got too close to her. It was a nightmare, but Betha forced herself to her feet. Forced herself past her exhaustion, because if she didn't move, her friends would die.

CHAPTER TWENTY

As Betha took her first steps, retreating the way they had come, Angie faded with her, and Carter and Eric stood side by side, forming a rear guard. They had to move, had to get back around to the big guns, had to get protected.

When the demons realized their retreat was cut off, they fell into a frenzy, either fighting to the death or trying to run into the woods. The Guard were closing in, encircling, and Betha's little group was currently the cork in the bottle as they tried to prevent the demons from escaping.

The plan was for them to retreat, to let the Guard close the circle and kill the stragglers, but that didn't look as easy now as it had when they had all discussed it. There just weren't enough Guards left, and there were too many demons. It was clear where the weakest part of the line was, and the enemy began to shift their focus to Betha's small core group.

Multiple doglike creatures headed toward them.

Betha was tired, but she steadied her gun and fired, aiming as best she could. All of her lessons were gone, her head was foggy, and she wasn't even close to hitting any of the terrifying beasts, but she needed to try. Maybe she'd distract one. She would not give up. The dark, ferocious shadow that was Angie stayed by her side, keeping things away as Betha slowly backed up. She didn't dare turn and run.

They would chase, and her friends would die.

"Fuck you! All of you! I closed it and now you're all going to die!" Betha yelled at the mob of frenzied demons.

Then one of the smaller demons headed right at her, only ten feet away. She took a breath, aimed, and fired three shots, the last in her clip. To her shock, she hit the doglike shape, causing it to stumble. A flash of bright white from Eric's sword turned the demon to ash. Eric glared at her. That look was enough to get her moving and focused back on the plan. She dropped the empty clip and loaded her spare, then moved to keep Angie between the demons and her. She would remember the plan.

She had to, or her friends would die.

More gunshots sounded, and she kept moving backward, away from the scene. She lost track of Carter and Eric in the melee with all the chaos, but Betha could see that, overall, the Guard was winning. Angie kept pace as Betha retreated, taking out anything that got too close to them. The shadows of fellow Guards fell over them as they made it to the tree line. Guard members moved forward, the reinforcement squads pulling in now to tighten the noose, letting the pair through the line they were holding. Carter and Eric were nowhere to be seen.

Angie led Betha away from the battlefield and toward the tents. The sounds of fighting broke off as they finally moved beyond the wall. Everything around them calmed down, but Betha didn't relax. She clenched her gun in her hands, which wouldn't stop shaking. Someone took her gun away and led her to a chair. The image of the demon turning to ash in front of her kept appearing. If Eric hadn't gotten there, she would have been done. She had stunned the thing, but her little gun hadn't done more than anger it. Eric had saved her life, and the brothers were still out there because she had frozen and forgotten the plan. She couldn't let that happen again.

ANGIE SHIFTED from her wolf form and grabbed an extra-long shirt that was offered her way. She then wrapped her arms around Betha, who was shaking like a wet dog. "We are safe now. It's okay." Angie did her best to keep Betha grounded and there with them. She could feel the stares as Guards trickled in from the battlefield. Most were overjoyed that the portal was closed. The mood was very celebratory, and a few moved closer. They realized from the nearly predatory look that Angie threw them that now was not the time to thank her and moved on.

Carter appeared and made his way over to the two of them. Eric wasn't far behind. Neither looked injured, though Eric had what looked to be blood on his right side.

"She is in shock, and I think her power might have drained her," commented Angie as they came closer. Eric moved to Betha's side, and white light filled his hands. Angie didn't let go but glared at Eric. "Whoa, what are you doing?"

"I'm just going to smooth things over a bit, soften it. It will help. She is low on energy. Don't worry, trust me." His voice was smooth, and it made her hackles rise.

Angie let him continue, but her eyes darted to Carter, who nodded. "Fine, just be careful. She hadn't seriously fought anything before. This was her first real, organized battle." Her voice trailed off, not liking that Eric might mess with Betha's head. Angie didn't know how else to help her best friend, though. And Eric was related to Carter—how bad could he be? He didn't keep his hand on Betha's head for long, only a few moments, and it did seem to help. Her voice had reached several of the Guards who had inched closer to see what was going on.

Betha stopped shaking and focused on the room. Angie slowly let her arms fall from around her.

"We did it, right? I actually healed the tear?" Betha asked.

Angie nodded. "Yes, you closed the tear and kicked ass doing so. We got this." She knew they had another portal to go, but a success was a success. They were making progress, and it looked like everyone was all in one piece. Well, at least the four of them were in one piece. Eric vanished into the healing tent once Betha had steadied, and she knew many hadn't been so lucky. From her viewpoint on the battlefield, she knew the losses had been rough. Shifters could take a ton of damage and heal.

The elves, trolls, and trolls didn't heal as quickly. She could smell the blood from the healing tent and did her best to block out the sounds of people moaning.

BETHA HAD DONE IT, she could do it again. Angie looked at Betha, and without words, they knew, as hard as this was, it wouldn't be easier next time. But now they both also knew that they could do what needed to be done.

CHAPTER TWENTY-ONE

"As some of you know, three portals have now been closed by the new Traveler. One that was just being created, and two others that were under Guard control. All known portals have been closed, and we are here to discuss what comes next." The human council head sat down at the table, having made his opening statement to get the war council session started.

"I would like to object to that statement." Justin and the rest of the council turned to look at the angel, Kellion. "I believe that there is a portal near my Haven. There have been reports of an attack on Red Kill—the town nearby—and Haven, the sanctuary that it is, has taken in survivors from that attack."

"As we have discussed, we are confident that those demons came from a now closed portal, Kellion. Now, back to the topic at hand," stated the human statesman.

"I am not confident in your assessment," interrupted Kellion again. "In fact, I believe that those portals at Site

A and Site C were there to make us feel secure. I would like Traveler Betha to see if she can sense anything near Haven. Given that she sensed one being created, it should be within her abilities. If she says it is clear, I will drop the issue." Kellion looked around the table at the various leaders, challenging them to reject his request.

Justin understood Kellion's logic. "I think Kellion is correct here. We have been playing this like a direct confrontation, and while I hope that these were the only portals, the smart plan would be to distract us with two nice targets while slipping through the back door. If Betha hadn't closed the one on campus, it would not have gone well. In fact, if she and her group hadn't been so close when it was being opened, it could have gone very badly. We only have a small force here; the rest are draftees in training."

Vincent nodded before jumping into the conversation. "Our oldest stories of demons talk of them being crafty. So far, they haven't shown that. I would expect more of them, and it is dangerous to underestimate one's enemies."

The head of the council nodded reluctantly. He clearly didn't want to believe it. Still, the council seemed to be unified in its support of Kellion. "We will have a representative talk to Traveler Betha," he said.

They all looked toward Kyra, but Vincent jumped in. "Just tell her to go check it out. No need to be so delicate."

Justin had to resist rolling his eyes. He knew where this was going.

Kyra glared at Vincent instead of the head of the

council. "As you know, Travelers are outside of the draft and are not under the council's control. We are independent and must remain so by the terms of the Accords. Kellion and I will discuss it with her."

Everyone around the table nodded and agreed, some grudgingly, but with no real leverage. As Kyra had reminded them, the Accords were quite clear on the matter. Since the authority of the council itself came directly from the Accords, there was no way to challenge them.

"Is everyone ready for the next order of business?" The head looked around the table before continuing. "We need to discuss how we are going to track down the demon opening the portals. Andrea? Is there anything you can add?"

"I have seen that to catch the person, we will need the help of the angelic realm," said Andrea. Unsurprised, everyone turned back toward Kellion. Justin was beginning to think this was a ping-pong match instead of a council meeting.

The council head frowned. "I have sent messages to the angelic world but have not received a response. It has been over a year since we have had consistent contact with the angels."

Andrea smiled at the head. "I know. We will need to send Traveler Betha to them directly." Both

Kyra and Kellion paled at this news.

The council head said, "That's impossible, as you know. Per the treaty, no one from here can cross without explicit permission."

Andrea cut in, "As Traveler Kyra stated, Travelers are

not bound in the same way as the signatories by the Accords. They are independent. And they are not native to Terra, in any case. That clause applies to those native to this world alone."

"That's following the letter of the law very closely, don't you think?" asked Kellion.

"I have seen that if she enters the portal, everything will get better. If she does not, Terra will be overrun," she stated matter-of-factly.

Kyra turned toward Andrea. "What does that mean? Does she not come back?"

"I don't know, but I would rather not test fate right now. The goddesses of fate don't seem to be playing particularly nicely with regards to Terra, and believe me, it could get a lot worse."

~

THE FULL MOON WAS OVERHEAD, but Betha didn't remember walking outside. The last thing she remembered was being in the bathroom and showering. Now she was outside under the bright moonlight. That presence that she had channeled near the tears in the veil was all around her. Warmth and fireflies swirled around her as she stood there. There was no fear.

While all of the Guard had been overjoyed at being able to downsize the two posts, Betha had been horrified. The number of brave Guard members who had given their lives so she could close those two portals was too high. That people would give up their lives for her was an emotional bomb that she wasn't sure she could handle right now. On the other hand, she had seen it on a massive scale, so whether she was ready or not, she had to at least acknowledge that people had, in fact, died for her. They deserved that recognition at the very least, and probably a lot more.

Betha felt safe, though, for the first time in days, here among the fireflies and moonlight. Her first battle had been horrible, and she had needed help off of the battlefield. She was fairly certain that Eric had made sure she didn't have night terrors from it. The second battle had gone better, following the same pattern, but closer to dusk. Feeling safe was such a blessing. It was almost like a hug from her mother. Before Josephine had forgotten who Betha was and where they were.

The knife was key. If she destroyed the knife, the demons would stop. Fireflies circled her head as she stared up at the moon, thinking. She had such a hard time reconciling that this was all on her plate. The fates had a sense of humor, truly, but she was doing her best to rise to the occasion. Or at least she was trying to and felt she was doing okay.

"I am a Traveler. I… I protect the leylines." Hearing herself speak those words brought forth a rush of emotion, but not just from her. It was there again, that feeling, or presence. It seemed joyful at hearing the words. She couldn't help but smile.

"At least you are happy that I am a Traveler. I don't know if I will be able to protect the leylines, but I will try with all that I have."

She reached for the warmth inside her and offered it up to the presence like it was a tear in the veil. They connected, and the images of stars filled her mind, along with the feeling of paper cuts all over her arms. Then it was gone along with the fireflies, and Betha was back in the shower, wondering what had touched her and what it meant.

CHAPTER TWENTY-TWO

Kyra had given Betha a call and asked her if she would go check out the area near a town called Haven. Haven was a hidden town that most people didn't know existed, and it was run by Kellion, the representative for the angels on the council. Red Kill, a nearby town, had apparently been attacked, and there was some concern. Kyra had emphasized it was an ask, not an order, but that if Betha agreed to go, it would be useful to her in future dealings with Kellion. Betha didn't really understand how a whole town could be hidden, presumably through some powerful magic. That was beyond anything she had thought existed.

Betha discussed it with Angie first, and her friend didn't have any objections. From there, she wanted to talk to Carter. She sent him a message and asked to meet at the picnic tables near the gym. He agreed, saying he'd be there shortly. Angie patrolled the area as Betha waited for Carter. It wasn't like Angie needed to be nearby to listen in to the conversation, and she knew her friend would have her internal ears focused on eavesdropping.

Carter walked out of the gym and sent a smile her way. He headed over to the picnic tables and took a seat across from her.

"Is everything okay?" he asked.

"I need your advice," started Betha. "Kyra asked me to check out this town called Red Kill and said that Kellion would look at it as a favor. He thinks there might be a portal nearby. It's near some place called Haven."

"If Kellion thinks there is one nearby, there more than likely is one," Carter commented. "I haven't known him to be wrong very often."

"Then we should check it out," replied Betha. She leaned back, wondering if they could find the knife this time.

Carter nodded. "I would appreciate that. Kellion is basically family to Eric and me. And Haven is a quirky place, but lots of good folks live there."

Now, this was interesting. "I am surprised he didn't ask *you* to talk to me then," said Betha. Betha knew little about Carter and his family. Only that Eric existed and had his wings and gifts, but Carter didn't.

"He more than likely knows we are working together, but since Kyra sits on the council it makes sense she'd be the one to ask. Eric and I both know the area around Haven well, though." He hesitated but continued. "We grew up there."

"Oh, so the opposite of me. I got the human suburb, and you got the magical hidden town. Do you still have any family there you'd like to visit?"

"Nope, we have that in common as well, you and I. I've only got my brother, like you only have Angie. Though, you are closer to Angie than I am to Eric."

Betha snorted. "Well, he can be a bit full of himself. I want to pop his head with a pin sometimes."

Carter laughed. "Believe me, I understand, but I trust him with your life. I take it you aren't interested in having him as an Anchor then?"

"Not at all." Betha said. "He wouldn't fit my family."

"Family?" Carter's look changed to one of confusion.

Betha blushed. "Well, I feel like my Anchors are my family. I mean, like you said, I don't have any other family left, and we are sharing parts of each other's souls. It's a chosen family, and a bit more permanent than most. Or that's how I think about it."

Carter stood up from the table. "It sounds like I need to plan a trip for us to Haven. I should get on that." He turned toward the gym.

"Ask him out before he gets away."

Betha was not prepared for that to run through her head. She didn't freeze, though. Not this time. She called to him just before he started walking away. "Uh, Carter?" She paused awkwardly. "How would you feel about..." Betha turned bright red. "Joining the family?" She'd completely messed up what she was going to ask. That was not the going-out question. Okay, maybe she did freeze. A little.

His mouth opened, and Carter looked surprised. "I am human, and I have nothing to offer you." He turned and headed away before Betha could come up with a reply. She couldn't believe that was his answer. She quickly got up to go after him, but Angie was there and held up a hand.

"You should give him time to get used to the idea. That was a big question, and I'm sure it wasn't one he expected. Heck, it wasn't the one I expected."

"You're right, plus we have a mission to get ready for. How about we have dinner with Joey and Ben? It will give the two of you some time since you won't leave my side." Betha shook her head, wondering if she'd blown her chances with Carter. She needed to get her priorities on track.

~

THEY WERE USING Kellion's town of Haven as a base, and the plan was to go out searching from there. Kellion stood next to Betha outside the door of the meeting room where volunteers were gathered.

"I don't know any of these people. Why should our team grow from the four of us?" Betha asked the tall angel beside her.

Kellion gave her a pointed look. "You will not have an entire squad of Guards with you. Sneaking around is your best bet, but you need more firepower than just the three of them can provide. Plus, these all were selected by the council. They are feeling a bit slighted because of your time on Luna's Pack lands."

Betha kept her reply to herself, but she really didn't want to be responsible for even more lives. Or have the council messing in her life. The push to take another Anchor was definitely being felt, but she knew it had to be her choice, and damn the council if they thought they'd get to choose instead.

Angie smiled as she came up beside them. "You have great instincts. Trust yourself. Just pick a few people, and Carter can give them a once-over to see if their skills will fit in the group, if you think that's necessary."

Betha nodded and entered the room. People kept talking and didn't really notice her. That suited her just fine as she looked people over and tried to feel anything about any of them. Her eyes kept darting to one lady near the wall who was carrying a sword. From training with Eric and Carter, she knew sword work was hard. It required dedication. She gave her a nod, and Angie started toward her in the crowd. Betha kept looking, trying to see if anyone else stood out.

Kellion entered the room, and the chatter died out. Her eyes went back to the group, but now everyone was watching Kellion, and it was harder to get a genuine sense of them. She walked around people to see if she literally felt anything, to see if her power told her anything about any of them.

One other person felt warm, like a very nice shower, when she passed by, and she tapped him on the shoulder. He was a giant, standing nearly seven feet tall, and built like a brick wall. From there she made one more loop, then headed toward the front. "That's everyone," she whispered to Angie. Betha darted out of the room before she could change her mind.

The whole team gathered in the hallway—Angie, the lady with the sword, Carter, and Eric. Add in herself and the giant man behind her, and it was too much. She was done. She really couldn't take responsibility for more than this.

"All right, this should be all of us. I am Traveler Betha. You can just call me Betha—the Traveler title is a lot," she said, and everyone smiled a little. Angie introduced herself and then motioned to someone else to go next.

The lady that Angie had been talking to spoke up. "Jessica, daywalker. I am great with a sword, and I am a protector in training." Betha wondered if Jessica was related to the dean of admissions, who was a daywalker. This must be the vampire representative, since daywalkers weren't limited to nighttime activities. Protectors were the best of the best vampire warriors.

Carter gave Jessica a nod, and Betha wondered if they knew each other. The brothers shared a glance and then Eric spoke up. "I am Eric, Nephilim, and this is my twin Carter, human. We know the areas that we are going to scout and hopefully find the tear. We are from Kellion's direct line, and we know the lands surrounding here well."

Betha almost missed the next person, since she was stuck on the fact that they were twins. That had to have sucked. Not only did your brother grow wings, but he is your twin, and you didn't. Not to mention, they're directly related to Kellion. No wonder they thought of him as family.

The last guy nodded. "Brutis. I am a cat shifter—an extra-large panther."

Betha connected dots she didn't even know were in her head. "Carter and Eric will take point since they know the area. Angie will proceed in wolf form, sticking to the shadows, hidden. Brutis, you will be with me in cat form. Jessica will take the rear. All agreed?"

Her normal group looked surprised, especially Eric. Carter gave her a nod and replied, "Brutis, I haven't worked with you, but your kind have a solid reputation. Keep Betha safe—you should have the advantage in close quarters. Jessica, you're one of the best vamps I've seen with a blade. Use it well, and we should do fine. The goal is to not run into any large groups of demons, find the tear, close it, and hold the location until backup arrives."

"That's if one exists. I love Kellion, but he can be paranoid," Eric piped up.

Betha frowned and shook her head, thinking back to her weird dreams. "I think there are several smaller tears nearby and that we are going to need to find them one by one. I'll know for sure once we are outside the walls and in the forest." At least it sounded like she knew what she was doing. She didn't feel like it, but she was quickly coming back to her old mantra. When all else fails, fake it 'till you make it. She could do this.

Carter spoke up, breaking the silence that had come over the group. "We will head out in one hour."

~

"Did you ever think that we would be in the woods looking for a portal to a demon world? I mean, I'm not worried, we got this. Three portals done and we will get this one closed as well. But still, did you ever think?"

Betha couldn't help but smile. Angie was completely right. This was not on the agenda for her first year at St. Luna's. No one in the group could see where Angie was in the shadows, and Betha was thankful that they could talk inside each other's heads. They hadn't had a ton of time to discuss the upgrades that Angie had gotten by becoming an Anchor.

"You're one to talk, miss sneaking around unseen," sent Betha.

Everyone paused as Carter and Eric froze, then motioned them forward. "Can Angie look around about a half-mile in that direction?" Eric pointed toward a hill near the side of the town they had been approaching.

They had left Haven around noon and had made good time. They'd taken some trails that had led to the town of Red Kill, since Haven wasn't on any map. In fact, if you didn't know to look for it and weren't welcome, Haven was virtually impossible to find due to Kellion's influence. It turned out to be not nearly as big as making the town invisible or anything, like Betha had imagined. Instead, there was just a subtle mental compulsion not to notice the area and to change direction to miss it. Angelic lines were powerful, and Kellion had said it wasn't a strain on his abilities to keep the town hidden.

"We think the demons came from that direction, based on what some survivors said. We know a bunch are holed up in Red Kill, and we don't want to go near it if possible. At least not before we close the tear," said Carter.

Betha nodded and passed the instructions on to

Angie. *"Be careful. We do not know how many demons would hang around town."*

"I'll be fine. I am staying in the shadows."

"Should we continue forward or wait until we hear back?" asked Jessica.

Carter looked at Eric before replying, "We shouldn't really stay here. There is a trail that goes in that direction. We are going to have to be quieter from here on out. The trail doesn't approach the town, but it gets close at one point. If I were in charge of their scouts, I would have them posted watching the trail."

"I found something," sent Angie. *"I think it's a trail, though I can't tell which way to go. It smells horrible, like rotting meat. I'm going to head back your way and bring you here."*

"Angie is approaching. She doesn't think there are any scouts ahead, but something smells horrible," said Betha.

Since Betha had warned them, no one jumped when the dark wolf literally walked out from the shadow of a tree. Everyone was on high alert as they made their way down the trail. Unfortunately, it was in single file, and Betha couldn't see anything, but it was quieter than if they had been walking through the brush. Betha could only walk semi-quietly, and she attributed that to the abilities she had gotten from Angie. Everyone else was silent, even Carter. It was humbling, trying hard to be silent and still being louder than the other five of them combined.

Brutis took up the rear in his panther form. He was bigger than Angie in her wolf form, although they both had very dark fur. It took so much willpower not to pet him the first time she saw him shift. His paws were gigantic. He was a giant black panther that was too big to be natural, and all she wanted to do was cuddle him.

It took awhile, but Angie led them to a trail that cut across the one they were on. Carter and Eric both looked shocked. Carter spoke up, "This wasn't here before the attacks. Angie, can you go that way for a short run and let us know if it's any different?" The trail looked like a blowtorch had cut through the trees and bush. The ground was covered in ash. Angie took off down the way he pointed.

Carter crouched down and touched the ground. "This has been burned. It's like a forest fire but guided. I don't know what could do this."

Eric looked confused before joining the conversation. "I don't know of any demon that could do this. It must have been more than one. It's like a slug made of burning embers came by or something."

"Slug made of burning embers? That's a thing?" asked Betha.

Carter shrugged, and Eric poked at the ash.

"Can you let them know the trail hits a road in this direction? I am on my way back."

"Angie hit a road and is on her way back. What is in that direction?" asked Betha, pointing the opposite way.

Eric shrugged. "That's the direction we were guessing had a tear. The question is, did this potential slug pass this way toward the road or go that way into the woods?"

"Tell him it headed toward the road. The road is still smoking."

"We are in luck. Angie said she thinks it's going down the road since the road is still smoking."

Carter quickly spoke into his comms, giving instructions to someone on the other line. When he finished, he summarized, "Since it went in a different direction, another team is going to check it out. We should investigate where we think the tear ought to be."

The path seemed to go on forever, and they discovered it did not go in a straight line. Instead, it twisted and turned all over the place. They passed by several other trails that Angie confirmed had been traveled by different demons, based on the various scents.

It was getting close to sunset when Betha realized she could feel a buzzing in her head. She held up a hand and everyone paused. "The tear is over there, off of this trail," she said after focusing for a moment. She pointed toward a hill that was away from the slug path. "Maybe the slug didn't come out of the portal?"

Eric looked thoughtful. "It didn't sound like one of the demons I learned about, but I don't know everything."

"Our first goal is to close the portal, now that we know it's there, and then call in reinforcements to guard it. Since the slug, or whatever it was, went the other way, let's just let it be for now, okay? I think we've got enough to deal with." She hoped it was the right call, and since no one objected, Betha prepared to do her part and close another tear.

CHAPTER
TWENTY-THREE

The awareness in her head had changed from a buzzing sound to something different. Now Betha knew what it was. Hopefully, it was a sign that she was getting a handle on her abilities.

"I think I found it, along with two demons," sent Angie.

Betha relayed the news to the group and knew exactly where she needed to go. "We need to be quick. Eric and Jessica, you two take point to deal with the demons. Brutis will watch my back as I head toward the tear. Carter, you're backup, and Angie can keep to the shadows in case they aren't the only two demons nearby."

The feeling of something wrong got stronger as she neared the bright clearing. She could now see the two demons, who were dancing around a fire, very excited by something that was burning inside. They were the first upright demons she had seen so far. Both stood as tall as she was, with short horns and tails. One was a dark brown color, and the other red. Betha recognized them as imps from her studies. Betha couldn't tell what was burning in the fire, but the smell of burned hair drifting across the clearing.

Her gaze went to a short cliff behind them with boulders on one side. She'd bet money that the actual portal was along the cliff face. It was like she could see a ghosted outline of where it should be. A line glowed in her mind, and the sense of wrongness got stronger when she looked directly at the outline.

Jessica darted into the clearing with Eric. Betha moved toward the cliff with Brutis. Angie was in the darkness somewhere, keeping an eye on all of them.

Both demons darted toward the cliff face, but when they saw the rest of the group, they paused. That was their mistake as, without warning, Jessica dispatched one, its head rolling across the clearing. The other attacked Eric with a screeching yell. Between Eric and Jessica, it went down quickly, but the forest went silent. Really silent. That yell had been very loud in the trees. No more birds cried in the distance, and everything fell eerily still.

Betha focused her attention on that glowing line in her mind near the cliff. Her goal was in sight.

"That was loud, really loud. Louder than it sounded, if that makes sense."

Betha ignored Angie to take care of the tear while Brutis circled the clearing. Carter took up a stance behind a pile of fallen rocks. Betha smiled as the tear glowed silver, then it trembled and fought her. "Shit! The tear is trying to open, to let something through!"

Bright light spilled out from the tear, and something darted into the clearing from the portal. It was bigger than the initial two demons, and it was fast. It was six feet tall—green, scaled, with horns and a pointed tail. Its face was vaguely human, but with the nose of a dog.

Betha wanted to throw up as a rotten stench emanated from the demon. She turned her back on it and instead focused on the line. "You are going to heal. Right now!" Her energy surged forward, and more light filled the clearing. Finally, the resistance crumbled, and the line slammed shut in her mind.

"There are more demons in the trees! Fuck, I didn't look up!" Angie voice caused her to glance upwards into the tree tops.

~

ANGIE BLAMED HERSELF. She hadn't searched the trees when she scouted the clearing. It was a hard lesson to learn, and now they needed to survive it. That tear needed to close, and Betha needed to survive.

As soon as Angie told Betha that there were demons in the trees, several more of the short furry imps entered into the fray. Thankfully, she could dart in and out of the shadows, taking down demons with her claws before vanishing to another shadowed spot. This was a perfect environment for the shadow wolf, and that might just give them the edge they needed to get out of this without losses.

Even so, the smell of blood and burned fur filled her nose and made it hard to keep track of where she was.

She did not want to bite any of the horned demons, if possible. They smelled horrible.

As the demons emerged from the tree line, they surprised Jessica and tossed her. Angie had to move out of the shadows to cover the daywalker's back until she was on her feet again. Jessica growled at a demon, fangs glistening in the light. Their team was not large, and with the number of opponents, they couldn't afford to lose anyone. Thankfully, Angie and Jessica were making progress on taking out the creatures from the trees, even with the sun in the clearing limiting Angie's ability to shadow-walk. Jessica moved even faster than Angie thought possible, using her sword like a master of old. Carter, Eric, and Brutis were each holding their own, whittling down the demon things that kept falling from the trees.

They were working well as a team. As the group attacking Angie and Jessica came down to the last few of the smallest, fastest ones, the demons took off into the woods. Angie turned back to the clearing. She could feel Betha's fear for everyone as things calmed down. Carter's gunfire was loud, and with every shot, another demon hit the dirt. Then, suddenly, a very human scream pierced the air, and it felt like everything paused.

~

THE TEAR WAS CLOSED, which was Betha's signal to hide and help as she could without putting herself in danger. Carter's gun kept going off, and Betha grabbed her pistol from its holster. Eric and Brutis fought the thing that had come out of the tear just before Betha had closed it. The demon was powerful, and while they were making progress with knicks and minor damage, it was taking time, which was wearing all of them down. Betha took a shot at the giant demon, and it turned toward her. That was the moment Eric needed, his blade glowing bright white as fire danced along its blade, turning the demon to ash.

The scream caused her to turn. Carter was on the ground with a demon on top of him. Betha moved faster than she ever had before, but Eric was already over his brother. With one smooth stroke, he removed the thing's head. With his other hand, before the body even fully fell, he shoved it off his brother to take stock of his twin's injuries. Betha didn't know what to do. Healing wasn't one of her powers, but right now, she wished it was. Carter was bled from his chest and stomach, the blood pooling around him in the clearing. The thing had broken his arm, and white bone poked through the skin.

"You will be fine, don't worry. You will be fine!" yelled Eric as he focused on stopping the bleeding. But it wasn't working, not as well as it should, and the bleeding was only slowing, not stopping. Betha crashed to her knees next to Carter. This wasn't a stable patient in the infirmary, and Betha could see that it wasn't good. Devastation was plain on Eric's face.

"Brother," Carter's voice came out in pain.

"We will get you out of here." Eric panicked as he looked around the clearing, his hands over his brother's chest. His power flickered only weakly in his palms since he'd used so much during the fight. Jessica's voice was loud, calling over the comms to get reinforcements to their location, along with a medic.

Betha whispered, “Carter, you need to stay with us.” His eyes flickered over to her, and he smiled.

“You got this kiddo. Best Traveler ever,” he said, his voice fading. Eric’s light flickered again, and he swore as it went out. Blood still pooled beneath Carter on the leaves.

“Betha, save him! Anchor him!”

Betha didn’t even think about it as her hands went to Carter’s chest. Power flooded her as she reached out. It flickered for a moment, and she didn’t know if she had enough energy for this after closing the portal. But she *had* to have enough. Carter had to live.

“No! He is worthy!”

Fireflies seemed to flicker around her hands, and the presence was back again. It nudged her gently as various memories of training with Carter flickered through her mind. Some of them were ones she wasn’t in, but she wasn’t given time to think about it. Then everything went black.

ANGIE FELT a jolt to her core, but her focus was on keeping the demons at bay. Most had fled with the death of the big one, but a few were still near the clearing, angling closer as they sensed the distraction of most of the team. She and Jessica were barely making progress against the stragglers, then Brutis joined them to finish off the demons that were left. Suddenly, white light flickered through the clearing, and the rest of the demons fled in terror. The three team members turned back toward the group. Angie's ears picked up the sounds of a helicopter making its way to their location, so she knew they would have help soon. The radio crackled, asking about the flash of light, and Angie guessed they must be closer than she thought.

Jessica responded to the radio, "That's us. There is a clearing!"

Angie looked over at the group surrounding Carter, catching the look of horror on Eric's face. He only paused a moment before his hands were back on Carter, healing whatever he could. The light in his palms glowed brighter than before. Betha frowned at Carter, her attention focused on his face.

"Betha?"

Eric's head turned toward Angie, his eyes growing wide, but Betha didn't move.

"Betha?"

Angie darted forward as Betha's eyes rolled back in her head. She stopped her from falling over Carter. Inside her head was a giant tangle of threads, and she couldn't understand what had happened. Then she, too, lost consciousness.

CHAPTER
TWENTY-FOUR

Betha stared up at the full moon in wonder. Fireflies danced around her to the sound of crickets. It was so peaceful and relaxed. It felt like home, like this was where she belonged. The moon slowly sank toward the horizon faster than she thought possible. True darkness crept over the sky.

Throb.

Throb.

Throb.

Her mark pulsed to the same beat as the fireflies. She turned her wrist upward and froze. The star had changed; it was now a compass rose, and the shadows she had gained with Angie were different. The swirls now had feathers at the ends. It was like a cuff tattoo wrapping around her wrist. Her power rose up within her, and she watched as the star shimmered with her light in the darkness.

The presence was all around her, and it seemed

better, stretched less thin. The clearing was more at peace, more content.

"I am a Traveler, and I protect the leylines."

The peacefulness slowly changed to joy, and the fireflies danced around her. Within the darkness, the fireflies glowed. The stars shone above her head. As she looked around, the stars made patterns, but different ones than those she knew. The fireflies weaved paths between the stars. The pathways that they were making seemed to make something, but she couldn't figure it out.

"I wish you could talk back to me. Someday."

~

BETHA WOKE UP IN A BEDROOM. Somewhere she didn't recognize, but it was warm and comfy. Someone had taken her armor off and cleaned her up. She hoped that it was Angie, given that she was in a long nightshirt with different underwear on. She could tell Angie was up and eating, though she wasn't the only one. It took a moment, but Betha realized Angie wasn't the only one eating. Someone else was with her, and they were both showing up in her head.

Angie, who was like darkness, and someone else—probably Carter—who was like gunpowder, and a third presence, who was like white lightning.

"Oh, fuck."

"Oh, fuck is right," answered Angie.

"It seems you saved my life, and made me an Anchor," added a male voice, who Betha was sure was Carter.

"And added me as well," said another very faint voice.

"Who is that?" asked Betha. She glanced around for something to change into. Having this conversation in her head was too much.

"Eric," Angie and Carter chimed in at the same time.

Betha's face turned bright red, and she was glad that she was the only one in the room. How do you accidentally turn someone into an Anchor? She crawled out of the warm bed to head to the shower. She definitely needed to be more awake to deal with this. Though, she supposed, that was one way to wake up—finding out that you basically changed someone's whole life by accident. The turmoil she felt inside was a bit much, and hiding in the shower seemed like her best plan. Hot water didn't judge.

The white lightning was a bundle of joy as it moved closer to her, and Betha did her best to ignore it. To her shock, there was a knock on the bathroom door.

"Now is not a great time!" Betha replied as she jumped under the hot water.

"I think now is the perfect time." The door opened a crack and Eric projected his voice into the room. "You didn't take the choice away from me about becoming an Anchor. I made the choice to do whatever it took to save my brother. I would gladly make it again. Becoming an Anchor is an honor. You didn't wrong me, Betha. You saved Carter. He was dying. You stopped that and made us both Anchors."

Betha washed her hair even faster. Being naked in the same room as Eric wasn't something that sounded like a great idea. "Great to know. Can I finish my shower in peace now? We can finish this conversation with everyone in a few minutes."

"I need to work on the head thing. I can't get it to work consistently with Angie. Carter I can talk with clear as day, but not Angie. I will wait. Once you are dressed, we can continue this conversation."

The door to the bathroom closed, and Betha took a deep breath. Frustration caused her to slap her hand against the tile. She did not want to continue the conversation, at least, not now.

"He isn't too bad, Betha." Angie reassured her. *"I think it just shocked us all since we didn't know it was possible."*

A few deep breaths later, and more than any sane person's share of hot water, Betha was feeling better. The feelings that were coming from the white lightning in her head were all good. The gunpowder was worried that she was beating herself up, and Angie was scarfing down enough food to feed an army.

After grabbing a towel, she poked her head out of the bathroom, unsure if Eric was in the room or the hallway. The connection wasn't like hers with Angie, and she didn't know why. He wasn't in the room. It gave her some time to get dressed and poke a bit at the connection in her head.

"Angie, I don't think he is fully an Anchor," sent Betha.

Betha could feel Angie set down the drink she had just picked up.

"We will be there in a moment."

Behind her eyelids, she could feel Angie and Carter move toward the room she was in. It was like a map, and they were glowing dots. Eric was a fuzzy thing. She could feel where he was but not like the other two. As Eric met up with Carter in the hallway, it was like she suddenly put glasses on.

Angie opened the door and looked at Betha, who was sitting on the bed. "Okay, what do you mean Eric isn't fully an Anchor?"

The concern on Eric's face was priceless, but Betha didn't laugh. This was really too important to worry about hurt feelings; they had to figure this out. The twins made their way into the room, sitting next to each other on the couch.

"I think when I made Carter an Anchor, Eric piggy-backed on the twin link since he was touching Carter. It's like it is half-formed, or it's coming through Carter."

The two brothers looked at each other, and they definitely had a conversation without the two girls.

"Guys, out loud, please," said Angie.

Eric frowned. "It would explain why I can talk to Carter with no problem, but I can't hook into the Pack mind, so to speak. My tattoo isn't like Carter's, either, but I just thought everyone's was different." He pulled his shirt off over his head and Betha blushed. His abs were just like Carter's, and she could feel the heat coming off her face. Yet the star on his chest paused her embarrassment. It was faded, not like the one on her wrist. It was not a six-pointed star.

Betha took a breath. "Carter, can you remove your shirt?" Her focus was on his tattoo, and the difference was staggering. Carter's six-pointed star was dark and almost seemed to glow. Feathered wings circled around it that seemed to move in the light.

Angie shrugged and followed suit, taking her shirt off. She had on a sports bra, but her tattoo was visible. It was like Carter's—a dark six-pointed star, but with shadows instead of wings.

"Yeah, I don't think Eric's is done," said Betha. Betha reached out toward Eric's chest but stopped herself before touching him. "I only have guesses, but I think you guys had a connection, and I strengthened that when I anchored Carter. So maybe you are partially anchored?"

"Could you finish it?" asked Eric.

Betha's breathing picked up and her palms felt sweaty. After she'd anchored Angie, she had slept for two days, and she did not know how long it had been since the tear had been healed. The thought of trying again scared her. And she still wasn't sure she really wanted Eric as an Anchor.

"I don't know," Betha finally said. She took a deep breath. "I had to move fast when Carter was down. There was resistance. I don't know if that is because Carter was dying or because you were in the link."

Angie pulled her shirt on. "How about you two get your clothes back on?" suggested Angie. Both guys slid their shirts back on.

"We can discuss this later. Betha needs to eat," said Carter. He grabbed his brother's arm and headed out of the room.

Once it was just the two of them, Angie gave Betha a hug. "Are you okay with this?" Having this conversation out loud seemed the safest. Betha was pretty sure that the brothers couldn't just listen in, even though her connection with Angie had definitely included eavesdropping. It seemed she had more of a boundary with the guys, even if she didn't understand why.

"Not really. I am not a fan of Eric. He puts Carter down and thinks he walks on water." Betha closed her eyes for a moment. "I think he could be an Anchor, but I am resistant to him. Like I told Carter, I want you guys to be my family, and I chose Carter. I didn't choose Eric."

"You don't need to decide now," replied Angie. "Are you still going to ask Carter out on a date?"

Betha laughed. "Oh fates. He probably knows. Today has been the greatest." Her voice came out high-pitched.

Angie patted her on the back. "We all survived, and we closed a tear. And both are thanks to you. We can't really ask for more than that. You know I love you no matter what. Whether you make Eric an Anchor or not, Carter has bonded to us—to you—and has no regrets. You'd know that if you'd bother to listen. It will all be okay."

Betha sighed. Life was complicated, but Angie was right. Carter felt solid, warm, and truly included. As for Eric, time would tell. And Carter was right about one other thing—she was absolutely famished.

CHAPTER TWENTY-FIVE

Carter glared at Eric as they walked away from the bedroom that Betha was using. They were in Kellion's giant house in Haven. They had put Betha in one of the guest bedrooms.

"You really put her on the spot," said Carter.

"You only say that since you are a full Anchor," shot back Eric. His face was red, and his hands were tightened into fists.

"I never would have asked for this, but Betha saved my life. I swear I died on that ground, but instead, here I am." Carter motioned to his body. His arm was still stiff, and he had scars on his chest where the claws had grabbed him, but he was upright. It was a miracle. "I was ready to give my life for her. Could you say the same?"

Eric hesitated, then his shoulders sank. "I am thankful that she saved you."

"Give it time. Let her see who you are as a person. Betha isn't just a Traveler; she is a person with feelings, and you can sometimes come across as an asshole."

Carter patted him on the shoulder. "I need to head back to physical therapy. All the shoulder rehab—you know how it is."

Eric watched him head down the hall. He could feel the sincerity coming off his brother. The bond between them was definitely stronger. They'd been close as kids, but things had changed when they had gotten older and gone different ways. Carter had gone into the Guard voluntarily, and Eric had gone to do his own thing. Now it felt like he had wasted so much time on being a flirt and partying. The fact that the bond was stronger excited him. He could feel his brother again. Still, he was frustrated, and he hoped Betha couldn't sense that.

"She shouldn't have had to save him," said Kellion from behind him.

Eric turned toward the doorway his grandfather was lurking in. "Aren't you a bit old to be eavesdropping?" This was not a conversation he wanted to have right now.

Kellion raised his eyebrows and crossed his arms. "Your job is to protect Carter. It always has been."

"Aren't you the one who wanted me on Betha's team? We are all supposed to be willing to die for her, right?"

"You know family always comes first. Always." Kellion's eyes glowed.

"Carter can take care of himself, and now that he's an Anchor, even more so."

"You both are Anchors, and you still have your duty."

"Mine isn't—"

Kellion cut him off. "As far as anyone is concerned, you are an Anchor as well. Are we clear?"

Eric turned in silence and stalked down the hall toward his own rooms, trying to keep the anger from showing to any of the new connections in his head.

EVERYONE AT HAVEN was celebrating the recent tear closing and that two more Anchors had joined the team. Kellion had an open bar, and all his soldiers had a rotation up so that everyone would get to spend some time at the party. Betha's Anchors were around the room talking with friends, and she was trying to stay in the shadows. She wore the smile everyone expected, but in her head was a maelstrom.

Angie caught her eye and approached with a curious look.

"What's up?" asked Angie. "I can introduce you to some folks so you would know more than us."

"It isn't that, though yeah, I know, like, no one here," said Betha. Her smile wavered in the low light. "We need to go back. I'm feeling unsettled."

Angie tilted her head in confusion, making a "please continue" motion with her hand.

The flood gates opened, and Betha rambled. "That wasn't the only tear in the area. I think there is a second one, which is why the demons still seem to be increasing. Plus, the outpost at the closed tear keeps getting attacked. Once we closed the last one, I swear I felt the faintest tug of another, but the Carter and Eric thing shook me a bit."

"Speaking of me?" asked Carter from behind them.

Both Betha and Angie smiled as he joined them. Betha couldn't help but give him a hug. "I am so glad you are okay. Don't scare me like that again!" She wrapped her arms around him tightly.

"Hopefully it won't happen again, but you know I am here to protect you, now even more than before. Did I catch something about another one?" asked Carter, pulling away.

Betha nodded and kept smiling as she noticed Eric making his way over. It was such a complex situation, and she disliked that she was in the middle of it. Everything she had read said this whole incomplete bond was impossible. He should be dead. Thankfully, he wasn't, but still, she didn't know what to do with him now.

"This is about that slug, isn't it?" joked Eric. Everyone turned and looked at him. Betha had completely forgotten about the potential fire slug. Eric actually looked sheepish. "I dreamed about it last night. That we were getting ready to go after the slug. Popsicles were also involved somehow."

Betha opened her mouth and then closed it. Instead, she nodded. She wasn't sure she could deal with a joking Eric.

Angie rolled her eyes. "Great, we get to go after a fire slug. And pelt it with popsicles."

Carter smiled and punched his brother in the arm. "I wonder if becoming an Anchor has increased your sensitivity."

The terrified look on Eric's face caused both girls to laugh. Betha couldn't help but wonder if any of Eric's powers had increased from being a partial Anchor. Angie had gotten some interesting upgrades—her ability to hide in the shadows had changed into being able to teleport through them. Before, she could vanish in a spot and hide, but now she could move through them. Carter now had a healing factor, healing faster than a human. They weren't sure what else had changed, and she hadn't really wanted to pry. Her own upgrades of greater speed, senses, and an increase to her own healing ability would come in handy more often than was maybe healthy.

"Well, at least you can keep up with me now," Eric fired back at Carter. He had a bright smile on his face. "I won't complain about it."

"Tomorrow let's head out and see if we can close another tear," said Carter.

Betha stared at him. "Are you back to mission-ready fitness? That last fight was a close thing." The concern in her voice was obvious, even if it hadn't also gone across their shared bond. Angie had discussed how to block emotions when she had been a Pack member, and Betha was practicing it as best she could, but it had only been a few days.

"I'll be fine. Promise," Carter replied with a twinkle in his eye.

~

NEXT TIME, Betha was going to need to specify when they were going tear and slug hunting. Eric and Carter had woken her up around 5:00 a.m. to get ready, and she would not have chosen such an unholy hour. It seemed they were on a schedule and wanted to get an early start to the day. She liked sleep, but in the end succumbed to their enthusiasm.

It didn't take long for her to get ready, though she was the last one ready to go. Even Angie was already munching on a breakfast sandwich when Betha made her way downstairs in her armor.

Breakfast didn't take long, then they were stepping back into the forest. As soon as her foot crossed the magical threshold, Betha froze. Five sets of eyes stared at her immediately, pulling out weapons. However, the most intimidating was Brutis in his panther form. He moved up close to her, his shoulder brushing against her hip, and Betha set her hand on his side to not fall over. His fur was as soft as she had imagined. It took her mind a few moments to catch up to why she had frozen.

"Well, it seems I got an upgrade. I know where the tear is," said Betha.

"Well, Kyra did say you would gain more abilities as you gained Anchors, and this was a two-for-one deal," commented Angie.

The magical barrier surrounding Haven must have blocked the call of the tear. It didn't take long for Carter to roll out a map and hand over a pen for her to circle the area. When she handed it back with two circles, his eyebrows rose.

"*Two* more?" asked Carter. He shook his head when Betha nodded.

"Yes, I don't think we can get to both of them today, but maybe. There are two very distinct ones," replied Betha.

Carter and Eric went over the map, plotting the way to go, along with if they should get some backup.

"The bigger circle is the one that has been open the longest. Even longer than the others we closed with the Guard," said Betha. The more she listened to the call in her mind, the more confident she became with her choice.

"You did get an upgrade," said Eric. "What does it feel like?"

The image in her head wasn't a pleasant one, and her words tumbled out. "It's like a wound that has been oozing for a few weeks. The smaller one is older still."

Angie padded closer to her and licked her hand.

"That was a gross visual," commented Carter. "Good thing we were up this early. I am going to let Kellion know so he can send some Guards over to the oldest one. Who knows how many demons are about. They are far enough away from each other that we can tackle the smaller one, and they can try to secure the other one."

Betha nodded at Carter, and Eric grinned. "Guess we aren't gonna tackle that slug today," he commented with some relief in his voice.

~

THIS TIME, marching through the forest didn't seem so strange. The further they headed into the trees, and the closer they came to the smaller portal, the more Betha studied the sound coming from the opening in her mind. It hummed. It was different from all of the other tears they had come across. For one, it felt older, almost like the portals at the Nexus. She tried to keep her eyes on her surroundings, but it was difficult with her focus on the tear.

Carter called a stop to the party, and everyone that was in human form gathered around. Brutis wandered into the trees, and Angie wasn't visible. "Betha, is it still in that direction?" He pointed off in the distance, which was not the direction the trail went in.

Betha nodded. "Yes, it is that way, which is of course not the direction of the path." Betha searched for Angie in her head and realized that she was farther away than she had assumed.

"Yeah, this path doesn't head back in that direction."

Carter frowned and glanced at Eric. "Do you think it's near the cliffs? We could detour that way. Otherwise we will need to hack our way through."

"Let me look." Eric backed away from the group, and his wings materialized from his back. He jumped upward and disappeared over the tops of the tall oak trees. The mark inside Betha's head that was Angie moved quickly back toward them. Jessica poked around the bushes on the side of the trail. Betha hadn't seen Eric's wings before, and they were stunning. Bright white, almost silver, with golden edges. She knew his armor had specific slits in them to allow his wings to appear. It was pure magic.

Then Eric's shadow appeared overhead, and he landed back on the trail. "Well, it doesn't look like there is anything for miles. I couldn't see any activity in the forest ahead, but you were right—those rocks that led to the cliffs aren't far."

"All right, we will head for the rocks, which will be easier than making our own trail the whole way there." Carter took point with Eric right behind him. Angie turned off into the trees before she caught up to them. Jessica took up the rear behind Betha, and off into the brush they went.

It was thankfully only twenty minutes of hacking through undergrowth before they came out to rocks that rose up ahead of them. Carter led the group out onto the rocky hill. "Betha, are we still on track?"

"Yes, I think it is along the rock ledge." The call of the tear wasn't far ahead, but the forest was full of loud birds. She caught a glimpse of Brutis wandering through the trees, along with glimpses of Angie in the spaces between the shadows. The hill didn't have much cover, and the group spread out instead of staying in single file. The climb wasn't very steep, but it was way beyond anything she had hiked before, and her calves burned. The tear was close, though.

"Wait," called out Betha. She paused in her climb, reaching out a hand to a boulder on her left. "It's like, right ahead, over there." Betha motioned in the direction they were going. It was more of a rocky climb. Angie darted ahead, a black shape against the gray and brown rocks. The bright sunlight made it hard for any shadows to form.

Angie's voice rang in all of the Anchors' heads, *"There is no one here. Nothing but rabbits and coyotes."*

Carter climbed up after Angie, and Betha followed. Jessica and Eric stayed behind as Brutis jumped after her. Betha grabbed Carter's outstretched hand, and he pulled her up a steep incline. Her eyes opened wide, taking in the view. They were above the treetops, and she could see several miles in every direction. As she looked about, the pull of the tear increased, and she moved around Carter and Angie.

"That is different," said Betha. The portal was near Angie, but it was smaller than she thought. It was only about the size of a person.

Betha slowly approached as everyone else paced on the rocks. The more she stared at it, the more she was certain this tear wasn't caused by the knife. "This must be a natural tear." She couldn't see through it, as it wasn't gaping. She poked at it with one of her hands, and the edges parted. The view of hell on the other side was yet another one. This portal was up high, and it looked like there wasn't a way to it from the other side. Jagged rocks rose up on the hell side. The sunlight was very bright, and nothing moved.

"Are you done staring?" said Angie.

"Sorry, it's different. It isn't accessible from their side." Betha gathered her power and barely touched the tear with it before silver spread along the edges. It sealed almost instantly. "That was quick." She turned to look back the way they had come. "Hopefully going downhill is easier." Now that she could see the way, she was less sure of how long it was going to take them to get back. The other portal was a dark red wound in her mind, and it stood out even worse now. "I don't think we are going to get to the other one today."

CHAPTER TWENTY-SIX

The war council filtered into the meeting room as people chatted. Justin took his seat and smiled at people. Kyra took the head of the large table, which was unusual. As she did, everyone settled down and took their seats. Kyra opened the meeting without any preamble. "Two portals have been closed near Haven, but another in the area has been targeted. The Guard are securing it as best they can before the Traveler takes care of it."

The council head nodded and took over. They motioned to the elven man at the table. "Yaz has begun to map the most likely locations where tears could be created. As we find them, we can close them. Each one closed is one less way into this world. Demons have attacked several additional cities across the area in a coordinated strike. Calls for help have come flooding in.

"The various species have been briefed, and their private forces are being trained and armed to help in this fight. The elves are going to be sending warriors, along with the trolls and orcs. Human volunteers are creating militias. The witches are providing back up support and working with the angelic lines to find what weapons work best. While bullets don't work on all the demons, they do work on some. Divisions are popping up learning sword fighting and coming up with additional weapons to try out."

"What of the Traveler?" asked Vincent.

Justin smirked. He knew Vincent was hoping that a vampire would bond with her. The last time that had happened, they had gained the ability to walk in the sun, creating another line of daywalkers.

Kyra turned toward the vampire. "She is growing. Another two Anchors have joined her. One of the angelic line of Kellion, and his twin, a human." Muttering around the table started up. "As she takes on additional Anchors, her power will continue to grow. I don't think she has even tapped into the beginning of what she is. Bonding to three Anchors successfully in a row is unheard of."

Andrea motioned for attention. The room fell quiet almost instantly. "My time as seer to this council will come to an end very soon. As many know, seers can't see one another, but the fates give us signs when our time of knowing is coming. I have seen the conclusion of this conflict with the demons. After it has happened, I will no longer be on the council. I don't know when my death will occur. If it coincides with the end of this conflict, I want to say that it has been an honor to serve with all of you. I take comfort that this conflict will end, and Terra will be victorious."

Not a sound could be heard in the chamber. Justin watched as Vincent began to clap, and slowly others followed suit, including himself. While Andrea wasn't the most loved member, she had provided valuable guidance and had been on the council longer than most. That her time was ending right around the end of the conflict wasn't good, and he understood why she was saying goodbye now. As he clapped, his eyes landed on the council head, whose smile didn't reach his eyes.

Justin's eye caught Vincent's, and he gave the elder vampire a nod. They would need to catch up afterward and discuss these recent developments. A seer leaving the council did not happen often, and it wasn't guaranteed that one would take her place. It would leave the war council in a tight spot. They would lose a significant advantage. Andrea was the last of her line, and the search for someone to provide trustworthy guidance was going to be tough.

CHAPTER
TWENTY-SEVEN

Josephine didn't mind being at Luna's Grace. Everyone was super sweet to her. It was hard when she had bad moments and couldn't remember why she was here. In her good moments, which were far between, keeping a journal was the only way things made sense. Josephine watched the news with the other residents, but the news was crazy. Tears were opening up and demons were attacking people and...something. She had a daughter. Betha.

Betha needed to know; she had to tell Betha the truth, and that was all that mattered before she forgot again. Her trip from the common room to her bedroom was short, and she gave a smile to everyone she walked past. Given the physical age of most of the residents, she looked like the youngest, but the truth was, inside, her very bones told a very different story.

Remembering her wonderful daughter was one of the few things that made it all worth it. All that she had to give up and let go. Her pen moved quickly across the page—these moments where everything was so clear were far apart. The words linked together on the page as she jotted down the why of all of this.

Our seer had foretold your birth. She knew Terra would need you. I willingly gave up everything so you would be you. It was worth it. You were worth it. I am sorry to leave this burden, but I know you will succeed. Whatever happens, remember Travelers are protectors of the space in between. We are sworn to protect it, and it protects the heart of hearts. You were born in between and can walk the darkest paths.

Josephine's pen paused, and she wondered how much she should write. While there was so much she had written within the pages, most of it was a scrapbook of Betha's childhood. The pain she felt when she thought about her daughter learning this truth, learning what she was, without her mother, was almost too much to bear. At least she only felt it during the moments she remembered. If she had known that it would be like this, she would like to say she still would have done what she had, but it would be a lie. One she would keep to herself. Not knowing how hard it would be for herself had been a gift.

Her hope was that the journal would make its way to Betha eventually. Though she knew it wouldn't until after she returned to the stars. The bound book wasn't much to leave to her daughter, but it was the most important gift she had. In every moment of clarity, she made notes, wrote to her sweet little girl. Though she wasn't a little girl anymore; she was a strong woman who would become one of the greatest. Everything she had done was with her daughter in mind. Everything.

Alarms sounded, and she paused in her writing. Josephine wrote one more line, then closed the journal and shoved it under her pillow. She moved to the door, confused as to why the alarms were going off. Yelling and screaming came from somewhere nearby. Panic overtook her, which was not the way to stay in the present.

She focused on her breathing to stay as present as possible as she peeked out of her door. People were running down the hall, and a healer was directing everyone to hide in their rooms. Everything in her froze as frightening creatures took down residents in the halls. Her breath caught in her throat as she saw one tear into a nurse she knew. Giant talons dug into the woman's back. Blood sprayed the walls. The beast had spikes along its spine and a spiked tail. Scales glittered in the flickering overhead lights. A dark figure was leading the charge. She couldn't get a look at the upright person, and her mark flared in pain. Josephine had a moment to hope that her mind would go so she didn't have to deal with this nightmare. Her mark shouldn't hurt—not anymore.

Instead, dread trickled along her spine, and she darted out of the room, away from the book hidden under her pillow. Her wrist throbbed, and her eyes widened at what she felt. It wasn't possible. It dawned on her what that meant, but it wasn't possible. All of the knives had been destroyed or returned home. Yet, he had one. This demon had one of the bones of her people. Not only that, it had belonged to someone from her bloodline.

Then the terrible truth dawned on her; the thing was here for her.

~

SOMETIMES BETHA DIDN'T UNDERSTAND why they were doing what they were doing. This car trip, for example. They were headed away from the fighting, yet she was heavily protected. The last tear that was near Haven had been easier to close than anticipated. Elven magic users had bombed the area, and then the Guard had dropped in with her group from helicopters to close the portal. She was very happy that they weren't taking another trip by air. They had found out the hard way that Angie got airsick. Now they were on their way north of the council lands. There was concern that there was a new tear that needed to be closed. The forest that they were driving through was similar to the area near Haven—tall oaks with the leaves changing now that it was late fall. At any other time, this would be a fantastic road trip with friends.

Thank the fates Betha was a people person. She had four constant shadows today. At least only three were in her head, and Angie was the only one who really talked to her that way. The guys seemed to prefer to speak in person. The group was learning how to not listen in to everyone else's heads. It took practice to talk to the person they wanted, and only that person. Still, she wouldn't give it up. It was a good way to communicate when her Anchor was in animal form. Jessica had also joined the party, representing the vampires and daywalkers. Betha didn't care about the politics, but she knew they were partly behind it. Jessica was at least a good companion. Brutis had something come up, so he was missing out.

Someone had lightly suggested that she look at Jessica as a potential Anchor. While everyone knew it didn't really work that way, anchoring Carter had definitely caused political drama, especially since he was human. That had never been done before, and people thought it was a sign of weakness that she had a human Anchor. Not to mention everyone thought Eric was an Anchor, and no one had anchored two people at the same time before, either. It was a mess.

"*Betha! Pay attention to the surroundings. Less on Jessica and more on what's going on,*" sent Angie.

Betha rolled her eyes. That a trip around council lands required all of her Anchors, plus Jessica, seemed a bit like overkill. Last time, it had just been just her and Angie. Carter had become more paranoid since becoming an Anchor. He took security seriously, but the fact that he had almost died didn't seem to bug him nearly as much as it should. That Betha had risked herself to save him bugged him maybe a bit too much. It had been nonstop drills since then, and pushing her to use every ability she had.

"*Betha, you are looking way too stern from here. Are you okay?*" asked Carter in her head.

Think of the devil and he talks in her head. Betha really hoped he hadn't caught her thinking about the drama of him being human. She understood that better than anyone.

Betha responded in kind, *"Just thinking about how we are on our way to the safe zone, and everyone has to go."*

"Are you guys doing that head thing again?" Jessica peeked around the car at the other folks. "I know you think you are sneaky, but your eyebrows move, and it gets really quiet."

"Sorry, Jessica. Everyone was wondering why I am annoyed that I need to have four bodyguards to drive five miles. Kyra doesn't have her Anchors with her all the time. And I don't even get to drive. Eric gets to drive, and I am stuck in the back seat."

"You are literally whining," commented Angie. "At least Brutis isn't with us." Betha glared at Angie as Angie elbowed her in the side. The car was on the smaller side, not as big as the one they had taken to the first tear.

"I am just worried about your safety. Think about how many tears you have closed and how many demons you have stopped from coming over to Terra. You are a prime target," answered Carter.

That Carter was worried caused her to blush, but she turned toward the window, hoping no one noticed.

"Are you sure that's why you are upset?" Angie asked. Betha could feel Angie staring at her. "You know why we are all here. So what's causing this? You aren't one to let something like this bother you."

Betha opened her mouth to reply but paused. Angie was correct—Betha did understand the reasons for the caution—so what was causing her to be prickly with everyone?

To her surprise, Eric piped up, "You need to work on meditating. You might have gotten some of my foresight sensitivity. It didn't even cross my mind that you might get some of that. We should start working on that in the mornings. Maybe just try talking for now?" Eric kept trying to engage her in conversation, but it usually failed. Normally he would chat with Carter instead, but this time he made a good point. While her emotions were a bit messed up with Eric, she wasn't sure that it was causing this whiny attitude.

"I'll try. I have a lot of random dreams, and they hint at the next day. I think I am being prickly 'cause it feels like we aren't making any progress. The main demon is still out there."

"With the knife," she added inside her head to Angie.

"And he can keep creating these tears," Betha continued to the group. "My dreams have been weird." She shook her head trying to clear her thoughts, then explained about the darkness and fireflies.

Sudden pain lanced up her wrist. "Oh sh—" Something plowed into the side of the SUV and shoved everyone sideways.

Carter's voice range out, "Everyone, brace yourself!"

Whatever it was hit the side of the car again, and Betha could see something on fire dart around the window past Jessica. The car skidded off the road and multiple glowing eyes shown within the trees. Carter fired out the passenger side window at the thing.

Eric tried to get control of the car but couldn't, and he slammed on the brakes. "Everyone out!" Smoke billowed out from under the hood as a demonic cat jumped up on it, facing them. Fire rolled toward the windshield.

Then Angie's door was open, and Betha followed her out of the SUV. Betha didn't have a weapon on her; they were in the trunk. She darted around to the back and tried to get it open. More fire came her way, forcing her to flee.

Carter was still firing, since he kept his gear on him. Demons jumped over the car toward them. Jessica darted forward with her sword, and Betha just watched in awe. Everywhere she looked, someone was fighting and kicking ass, and she was just standing there. Angie dove back in the car for a moment.

"Catch!" Angie tossed Betha, her sword toward her before shifting into her shadow wolf form, shredding her clothing. Then she vanished, heading toward the cluster of demons.

Betha held her ground as another cat-like demon headed her way—a creature with scales and a spiked tail. Panic overtook her; while she was okay with a sword, she wasn't that great. She still wasn't too far past "stick them with the pointy end." Her mind flashed to Eric, who was fighting nearby, his own sword glowing white, turning demons to ash with the smallest of cuts.

Now would be a great time to pull that off.

"Think of something amazing and perfect, then focus!" shouted Eric.

The fireflies from her dream came back to her as she swung at the cat demon. For a moment, she thought she saw a flash of white. The cat dodged the strike, but that momentary flash gave her enough confidence to attack instead of defending.

A demon hit her from behind, and it was all she could

do to stop herself from falling on her own sword. A black blur hit the demon that had knocked her over, but the cat demon in front of her charged. Betha tried to roll away, but it sliced through her jacket. The taste of blood filled her mouth as she bit down on her tongue.

It kept coming at her. Her mind filled with anger, and she focused on her power. To her shock, when the cat hit her again, it flinched back and rolled on the ground, trying to put out white flames. It screamed as the fire slowly turned it to ash. Demons retreated as the Anchors pressed forward, gaining the upper hand. It didn't take long for the demons to vanish.

Betha's gaze went back to the ashes. *I did that...out of anger?*

CHAPTER TWENTY-EIGHT

The target was glaring at her, or at least it felt like that. All Betha needed to do was consistently hit the target with bullets. There were moments of clarity, and she needed them to come about more often. It was like a part of her knew how to do it, but the shape of everything was wrong. The working theory was that Betha had gained some of Carter's muscle memory from his training, and now she just had to get it to sink in. It was his power, so to speak, that she could use.

"Keep your eye on the target and gently squeeze the trigger." Carter's voice was a perfect blend of guidance and encouragement. Ever since they'd bonded, he had been pushing her forward and trying to stretch her abilities as much as possible. While he still worked with others, his focus was on her. Betha hadn't ever eaten this healthily or been in as great of shape. The upgrades from Angie were now being put into use, as she was much faster than ever before. The angel fire from Eric was still sporadic, and only came when the need was very great.

Or she was pissed. Betha and Angie wondered if that would change if she chose to make Eric a full Anchor.

Bullets flew toward the target, near her intended area but not close enough.

"You are making good progress," said Carter.

Betha flashed him a smile but moved on to the next target. She had stopped blushing at his encouragement a few days ago. Any attraction she had, she buried as deep as she could. Concern flashed through the bond, and her eyes went to Carter. He wasn't watching her performance any longer. Someone else was approaching, and Betha was sure he was flying.

"*Looks like the council wants to talk,*" sent Carter to her.

"*Any ideas, Mr. Know-it-All?*" replied Betha. She wondered what this was going to be about. Hopefully it wasn't a conversation about Jessica.

"*Not on this. If I knew, I would have warned you he wanted to chat.*" He opened his mouth to continue out loud, but he didn't have time to respond.

"Carter! Good to see you, grandson." Kellion wrapped Carter in a big hug and then turned to look at her. "Traveler Betha." He held his hand out to her. "It is good to see you again. Today I represent the angels on the council." Betha's gaze flicked to his hand as she slid the safety on. "Thank you for closing the portals near my home, Haven. We have been hunting the remaining demons down and we can now send additional help to other cities and towns."

"You are welcome, though that is what Travelers are supposed to do."

"I have learned that just because someone is

supposed to do something doesn't mean they will. How about we go for a walk? We have something to talk about."

Betha knew it wasn't a request—she needed to keep the council happy. "Sure." She set her rifle down on the rack and motioned the council member onto the path. "So, what brings you to St Luna's, besides thanking me for doing my job?"

They both started down the trail, and it surprised Betha not to hear Carter walking behind them. She shot a glance over her shoulder at him as he started putting the guns away.

"You got this. I am only a thought away if needed, no matter what. Kellion can be difficult, but he isn't mean," sent Carter.

"The council wanted to discuss something new that the seer brought to the table. Something that involves you," said Kellion.

"*Seer?*" asked Betha silently to Carter.

"A person who can see future events. Andrea sits on the council. Kind of like Eric, but she can control it to a much greater extent and see and understand full visions," came the reply.

"Andrea, the council seer, saw you going through a portal to the angelic world in the next few days," Kellion continued, unaware of her quick clarification with Carter.

"I mean, just because someone saw me go somewhere doesn't mean I need to. Free will and all that," replied Betha.

Kellion laughed, but it sounded forced. "If it was only

that simple. If you don't go to the angelic world, she then saw the demons overtaking Terra."

Betha stopped walking and stared at Kellion. He looked way too calm to just have said that they could potentially lose this war. She wouldn't let that thought dwell in her head. Standing in the sunlight, he looked like a perfect statue. Didn't angels give people hope? Advice? Or even inspiration?

"Is that possible? Can a seer see potential outcomes?" asked Betha out loud and inside her head.

Several voices sounded in her head at once but then they went quiet. It took a moment for her to realize that Kellion was still speaking. "...and given that you are now bonded to Eric, it should be easy for you to travel there. The goal is to ask for additional support or soldiers. You will need to hasten with the time difference."

Betha held up her hand to get him to stop talking. "Whoa, hold on here. You want me to travel to the angelic world, ask for help, and there is a time difference? I think you need to start at the beginning and loop in my Anchors." Not to mention Kellion knew for damn sure that Eric wasn't one. At least, not fully.

Kellion turned to look at her, and he gave her a soft smile. It was like he could hear her thoughts racing. "Your Anchors couldn't survive the crossing. You will be the only one going through the portal."

Betha felt two of her Anchors walk within eyesight. Angie and Eric had been training separately, but it seemed that they all wanted to speak about this in person.

"What can't we survive?" Eric's voice drifted toward the two of them, and Kellion huffed.

"Ah, Eric. Crossing to the angelic plane. As you know, only purebloods can cross, along with Travelers, of course. No realm can prevent them. Even you, as close as you are, wouldn't pass the test."

Eric moved in front of Betha protectively. "Why aren't *you* going, then?"

Kellion frowned, taking in the situation. "If I go home, I violate the Accords. As you know, a full-blooded angel must remain on Terra per our signing of the Accords. It was one of the requirements for our people. Breaking the Accords would be a huge mistake. It would make the demon invasion look like child's play. The Accords must stay in place."

"So you want Betha to go instead and potentially lose a few weeks in transit?" asked Eric.

"We need help fighting the demons. You have closed enough portals to give us breathing room. The seer saw her going, and that it will cause enough of a change that we win. Is that not a good enough reason to go?" Kellion looked between Betha and Eric. Angie circled behind him, keeping him in the center of the Anchors.

"What is up with losing a few weeks? I want to know more about that," asked Betha. Eric motioned for Kellion to answer.

"It has something to do with how far away the world is," Kellion said. "The farther away it is, the longer it takes to go from here to there. Traveler Kyra would have a better explanation. I'm not a Traveler, so I don't really understand the portals; no one who is not a Traveler really does. The heavens are not as close as hell; it normally takes a week to get from here to there. In addition, a day isn't a day over there. Time passes at a different rate. Basically, you don't want to lollygag when you are there."

"So I head through the portal, let them know demons are attacking and we need help, then dash back here."

"In the strictest sense, yes," Kellion replied.

"It can't be that simple, can it, Eric?" asked Betha silently.

"No, it's not. The angels have rules, one of which binds him here," answered Carter. Eric must have passed the message along.

"What am I going to find on the other side of the portal?" Betha asked Kellion.

"A waiting area and a gate. Warriors guard the gate and will escort you everywhere. They can't harm you. To do so would provoke a war with the Travelers, which even they couldn't win. This trip should be easier than closing the tears near Haven since there won't be any demons."

Betha gave a nod to her Anchors, and they all took a step back. Kellion watched this with interest. She didn't see a way out of going. If this seer thought it was the only way to win the war, it might be the only way. It would take a few weeks, but that was better than sitting around waiting for tears to open.

"Fine, I'll go," she said.

Betha needed to talk to Eric. Especially before she went through that portal. Carter wasn't freaking out, but he and Angie had their heads together talking about security and their next steps. They were all around the table in Angie's room. Eric was trying to find anyone he knew who had gone to the angelic plane and come back. There was truth in the fact that even with his bloodline, it wasn't enough for him to go. It was a part of the Accords. Only purebloods could use the portal to the angelic plane. Travelers were exempted because no one could prevent them from using any portal they liked.

"Eric, can we chat?" asked Betha. He turned toward her and said goodbye to whomever he was on the phone with. She motioned him to take a seat near her on the bed. "We should probably talk about you being an Anchor."

The chatter from Angie and Carter paused.

"I don't want to be an Anchor unless you want me to be one," he said quietly.

Betha held up her hand for him to stop talking. "I am not being pressured into this. You stood up to Kellion for me today. We all saw it." She took a deep breath. "Honestly, I am scared. I don't know how to fix the bond. With Angie, it was so easy. We have always been so close. With Carter, I thought he was dying, and that was not okay. I didn't even ask, and you got sucked in."

Eric leaned closer to her. "I'm scared too. Carter can practically see into my head, and I know that you and Angie will be able to as well. Even though I am scared, I know that you won't use my thoughts against me and you can't possible die at this point. You have been dealing with everything fate has been tossing at you like a champ. All we can do is try."

Betha smirked. "That is true." She wrapped an arm around his back and leaned against his shoulder. "I really hope you don't die if we try this."

"Me too. Dying would not be a great look on me. So I'll try not to. But also, this is important, and I want to help. If this is what you want, for real, then I'm ready whenever you are."

With her other hand she reached out and touched his chest. She let her hand rest right above the tattoo he had shown her earlier. She gathered her power and reached out to Eric. White light spilled from her palm and overtook the room.

THAT SCREAM, it was Carter's!

Eric flew above the ground, his sword decimating the demon looming over his twin. There was too much blood. He tried to gather his power, but he had spent too much fighting the demons. Only a trickle worked its way into his brother's dying body, trying to heal the worst of the gaping wounds.

"You will be fine, don't worry. You will be fine!" It wasn't enough—he was going to lose Carter.

"Brother," Carter's voice came out weakly, painfully.

"We will get you out of here!" Eric panicked as he looked around the clearing, his hands over his brother's chest. He called out inside his head to the fates to do something, anything to save Carter. He offered to switch places.

He watched as Betha reached out and light flickered around them. Something tugged at his heart, and he gave everything he had. All that mattered was that Carter would live.

The memory changed shape, and Eric huddled with Carter. Both boys were crying as small wings peeked out of Eric's back.

"It doesn't matter. We will always be brothers. Twins forever."

The boys kept repeating the same ten words, holding onto each other in fear that the words would not be enough.

CHAPTER
TWENTY-NINE

It was done. Three dots blazed behind her eyelids, and she could feel Eric just like Angie and Carter. She kept the flashbacks to herself in that spot in her mind she discovered was only hers. Betha took a deep breath. She didn't want to do this, but she had to. They needed the angels to win this war. Right now they were doing the best they could, but eventually their luck was going to run out. Seven tears had been healed, and it felt like the demon opening them was having trouble finding places he could cut open. But still, Betha somehow felt it would get worse before it got better, and that only confirmed what the seer had seen.

Guards were stationed at every place a tear had been closed to stop any from being reopened. They knew from Kyra that since the demon wasn't a Traveler, he couldn't just open them anywhere. It was only locations where the two worlds were close. It seemed he was running out of easy targets.

Betha was trying not to drag her feet while she did

this. The Nexus was amazing, and she wished she was here to practice some more and not go through a portal. The portal in front of her glowed briefly in the light, and she looked around at her Anchors. Only Angie and Carter were here; Eric was outside with the Guard.

Kyra looked at Betha. "Moving through the Nexus is easy—I ground it at both ends so you just walk through. The heavens are different from Terra, and it's hard to stay there for any length of time. It's difficult to describe, but the light moves weirdly. As a Traveler, especially with Eric's bond, you shouldn't have any problems staying for a few hours. Remember—move quickly through the portal, state the problem, then head back through the portal. Time moves differently there, and you don't want a month to pass here by accident. You got this! It shouldn't be hard, and if keeping the Nexus open wasn't so important, I would go." Kyra's frustration was easy for anyone to hear. She stepped back to give Angie and Carter room to say good bye.

Betha reached out to Angie and gave her a powerful hug. "I will be back before you know it, and with help."

Angie nodded, and tears prickled Betha's eyes. She really wished that one of her Anchors could go with her, but that wasn't how fate worked.

"I know you will be back. Try not to be gone too long. All the testosterone will get to me," Angie replied. Betha smirked.

"Spend some time with Joey, I know you miss him," Betha replied.

When Angie pulled away, Carter gave Betha a quick hug. "You have this. We will wait for you. Plus, just think how much you can rub this in Eric's face. You get to go to the heavens, and he has to stay behind." She gave Carter the smile he was looking for. "He has wanted to see them since his wings came in."

"True. I hope he doesn't get his panties in a twist too much. Just be careful," Betha replied. She squeezed his arm as he pulled away.

Angie was going to be helping the Guard, along with Eric. Carter was going to be here to relieve a few Guard members from the Nexus. Everyone knew what they were supposed to do, and now she just needed to do her part.

Betha turned toward the portal before her courage ran out. This was harder than facing her first battlefield. Part of it was the time difference. She did not know how long this was going to take, and that bothered her greatly. Wrapping her head around the idea that a few hours for her was going to be weeks for her closest companions was difficult.

"I got this!" she announced, then darted into the light before anyone could respond.

Bright, blinding light. Dry heat. Everything was white.

At first, each step forward was like Betha's skin was peeling off. The heat worked its way into her mouth and down into her core. As it hit her, her power rose in response. The two met, and suddenly it wasn't so bad. It was like moving in slow motion. Each step forward became easier until things were normal. Something tugged her forward. The bright light faded, and she could swear fireflies surrounded her.

The path lay before her, but she looked around into the darkness. The tugging kept her on track, but she could see different doorways into other worlds. Each was like a star in the dark sky. Kyra said she should pop right into the heavens; she hadn't mention a path. Or a star-filled sky.

It was so beautiful and somehow familiar.

The tugging pulled her forward, keeping her on a path that was only slightly brighter than her surroundings. The doorway that it connected to was so bright she could not look directly at it. Her eyes darted every which way, taking in the darkness and the stars, keeping the end goal only in the corner of her eye.

Time didn't seem to speed by, but suddenly, she was in front of the door. Now she needed to walk into the light. This had to be done—they needed help, and she needed to stay on task. The doorway wasn't like the path. As she touched it, the light became sticky. It was like syrup, sticky and thick. Somehow, Betha knew it didn't want to let her in.

"Let me in! I am a Traveler," she whispered.

Each inch forward was a struggle, and her frustration built. This was taking too long. She didn't know if the counter was already ticking days away back on Terra.

"You will let me in!"

Betha yanked on her power, her thoughts moving to Eric and the white light he had. In front of her, the doorway quivered. It was enough to give her a shot of hope, and she gave it all she had, pushing forward. Then the resistance was gone. Her knees crashed to the ground, pain shooting through her legs. The air was too heavy and the light was weird, just like Kyra had said it would be.

I can't breathe.

It took a moment, but the pain stopped. The light seemed to get better, and she realized she was on her knees. It took several seconds for her to focus on her surroundings. The air was so thin, but that burning was still inside her lungs. Kellion said a gate would be open in front of her and that guards should be right there. That she would be taken inside immediately.

But no one stood next to the closed gate. He warned that the crossing was just to a meeting point. Everything was still, not a sound but her own harsh breathing. The air was too warm, and she knew she would be light-headed soon.

"We need help..." Her voice came out as a croak as she looked up, but no one responded. All around her was empty. Panic and anger filled Betha as she tried to stand. The goal was to keep her breathing even so she didn't pass out. Pulling herself up was a slow endeavor. Each breath took more effort than the couple before it. Her legs shook with each step toward the gate, but she had to get there. Someone would be on the other side. They had to be.

They are supposed to be here! Why aren't they here?

She wasn't getting enough oxygen, and the edges of her vision went hazy, but she kept moving toward the gate.

Then she was on the ground looking up at the gate and a bright blue sky. It was all the same—no sounds, no nothing. No way forward. Standing up a bit more slowly, she realized there was no way to even open the gate. No hinges, no lock. It was a solid block of metal. She couldn't help it as she tried to yell in frustration.

Betha grabbed the gate but flinched back almost immediately. The heat was too much for her hand, and everything inside her screamed not to touch it again. Betha paused, staring at her hand. Her skin was glowing like a lamp set on low.

Glowing skin like a firefly would not help. They needed help, and help wasn't coming, not from here. Betha needed to get back—time was ticking. She needed to go back through the portal. How much time had she already lost?

CHAPTER THIRTY

Angie was doing her best not to worry. Betha had walked through that portal only twenty-four hours ago. Everything was fine. This was the first moment she had to relax in what seemed like forever. The last time was when she and her friends had been studying around the table outside the café on campus. Life was so very different now. She had admitted to Joey what she felt for him after his injury. Now, she had some time to spend with him, on Betha's orders.

Based on his schedule, his physical therapy session should end at any moment. Angie perched outside the physical therapy office, leaning against a wall. Anxiety rolled around in her stomach with so much unknown, including how he would react to seeing her. She had kept in touch with him via dumb memes and simple messages, but that was all.

The door opened, and Angie froze. Give her a battle any day—it was better than this. Joey walked through the doorway, his head turned, talking to someone still in the office. Her heart squeezed at seeing him upright. Eric had done a pretty good job with Joey's foot, but it hadn't been clear if he would be able to walk again, in human or dog form.

Joey's head snapped around mid-sentence, and his eyes met hers. "Angie! What are you doing here?" He rushed forward, still being careful with his foot. She couldn't help but open her arms, bringing him into a hug. This was certainly better than her worst-case fears.

"I had some time off and wanted to see you," she muttered into his shoulder. Joey was okay. He even smelled the same, and part of her trembled.

Joey pulled back first, blushing. "I can't believe you're here. Can you tell me all about what's going on? You have been cagey in your messages. With how people talk about you guys, it's like you're superheroes."

"I will, I will. Are we still good?" asked Angie hesitantly.

Joey blushed deeper. "Of course. Let's go find somewhere to talk." His hand gripped hers, and she couldn't help but smile.

~

THE WAITING WAS GETTING to him. It was only supposed to be a week. Once the fourteen-day mark passed, Eric didn't give up, but he was losing hope. He wasn't the only one. The same day Betha had gone through the portal to the heavens, a tear had appeared in the city near Pack lands. The city was in absolute chaos.

For the first few hours, demons roamed everywhere.

Since then, the Guard had created a perimeter and was holding the tide as best they could. Eric was doing rounds with the Guard since Carter was guarding the Nexus. All the Anchors kept in touch, and it was shocking to find that the distance didn't matter; they could still mind-speak no matter where they were. It was one of the few perks they had.

Eric landed on the building roof and headed toward the door. It was time for a shift change, and it was his turn to do a loop on foot. He nodded to the two Guards near the door before heading down the stairs. It didn't take long before he saw the group that was gathering to head out. They kept Guard members on the roofs keeping a lookout and had others on foot doing patrols. It was all they could do to keep the demon population in check. This location was doing much better than the other across the city.

The group did a quick round of introductions. They paired him up with another of the angelic line named Susan. She was kind of cute.

"I guess we will be bait for this evening," said Susan as she caught his eye. Her voice was silky smooth, and Eric smiled and nodded. The first group out always had the horrible nickname, but the foot patrols helped flush the demons out. Between the two of them, they would be fine.

The first six blocks, they chatted a bit about nothing. Their voices were pitched to carry just ahead to get anything in hiding to come out. The full moon shone, and overall the weather was pretty good. If they weren't out on the street hunting demons, it would have been romantic. Eric kept his senses alert and his sword in his hand. Susan carried a rifle, but he could tell that they had drafted her, and she wasn't a regular member of the Guard. She didn't have any patches on the shoulders of her armor.

"So what were you doing before the world came crashing down?" asked Eric.

Susan paused for a moment. "I am a business major doing an internship on campus." She shrugged. "Just doing the college thing, what about—" She paused, and Eric looked over at her. He froze—her eyes had gone completely white.

"Susan." Eric reached out to grab her shoulder, but before he touched her, she flinched. "Whoa, you okay there?"

She looked around the building frantically and then got down on one knee behind the nearest car. "A group of demons are going to come down the street." The tip of her rifle pointed in the direction. "It looked like three or four. You might want to call it in. We have maybe five minutes."

Eric's mouth hung open, and he just stared. She was like a completely different person.

Her eyes flicked back to him. "You might want to hide, or you can play bait. I didn't see which would be better."

He was still stuck on the fact that she just had a vision, but his brain kicked in again. "Base, we have some movement on Green Street," he whispered into his comms. He moved to the other side of the car. "I thought all the folks with seer abilities were being pulled in with the council to find a replacement...” His voice trailed off as he saw something move down the street.

“Yeah, no...no one knows,” said Susan.

A minute later, four demons came out of an alley and headed down the street toward them—three cat demons and one that walked upright. Until now, no one had seen any higher-class demons in the city, only the animal classes. They would need to report this if no one from the roofs did.

Susan gave him a nod, and he grinned. It was time to rock and roll. Gunshots barked out as she took aim at the upright demon, and Eric darted out. His sword sparked white and glowed with angel fire. The cats headed his way, and it was nothing to get a deep enough cut in on each to turn them to dust. It seemed he had gotten an increase in his strength from becoming an Anchor. His momentum kept him moving forward in time to spar with the last demon. It had to be at least six and a half feet tall with broad shoulders. It wore some sort of clothing like a skirt, and its eyes glowed blue in the darkness.

The blessed bullets slowed the bigger demon down but weren’t enough to do it in. Eric struck at the creature, but it dodged. It struck back with its talons, but Eric moved out of the way. Susan kept taking shots as she was able, which kept the demon on his toes. Then she took out the creature’s knee. It stumbled forward and reached out to catch itself. That gave Eric the opening he needed to cut off its head.

“Well, that was interesting,” commented Susan. “Was that a higher-class demon? I think that was a first.”

"It was, and it was something new. New right now isn't a good thing," said Eric. So far, all of the demon attacks had been by those that were more like animals. While a few had been upright, like the giant demon near Haven, none had worn clothing. The more they looked like humans, the higher up on the totem pole the demon was. He frowned as he looked down the street before using a reporting the incident through comms. Once that was done, he started walking again on the route they were supposed to be taking.

"You just saw that, and no one knows you are a seer," Eric prompted.

Susan climbed to her feet. "I got a real bad feeling about the seer recruiting effort and said nothing when people were asking. My bloodline is weak—I am maybe 1/16 angel. I am nowhere near your power scale. The seeing stuff, it used to be really small. Only feelings, like a gut reaction. Right before the school year, it started to get stronger. Now I'm here, and I dreamed last night that I would tell you, which was weird 'cause I almost never see myself."

"Me? Why me?" Eric was confused but reached out to Carter to give him an update, along with the info on Susan.

"*Well fuck. You said she had a bad feeling about going with the council?*" replied his twin. "*Andrea's days are coming to an end and the council is looking for a new seer. Maybe she is the new bigwig, but if the council is bad news, then that isn't good.*"

"*One emergency at a time,*" commented Eric silently.

"Just so you know, you get weird expressions on your

face," chimed in Susan.

"I was talking to my brother about this. He mentioned that the seer on the council is 'dying'," said Eric.

Susan clenched her rifle even tighter. "Yeah, I don't know about that. My dreams with her in it are not pleasant."

"For now, let's keep this within the Anchors. We don't answer to the council." He watched as she nodded, though her face remained grim. He couldn't help but wonder what else she had seen.

~

CARTER WOULD NOT LOSE HOPE. He was one of the few Guards at the Nexus. Anchor James was there as well, and Kyra was nearby. They were prepared to lock down portals as needed. They had evacuated as many people as possible who had other worlds to stay in for the time being. Thankfully, the demons hadn't attacked the Nexus directly.

He should have said something to Betha before she had gone through that freaking portal to the angelic realm. Instead, he had given her a hug and acted like it wasn't a big deal. Now, more time had passed than anyone had predicted, except for the true pessimists. Betha could do this. Though he had realized—and hoped he was the only one who had realized—that Andrea hadn't said Betha would come back, only that she would go. He hoped he was wrong about that. More than just an Anchor or a friend would hope.

CHAPTER THIRTY-ONE

Betha stared at the portal. The actual traveling wasn't bad, but she didn't want to go through that gate again. That pushing-through-syrup feeling had been horrible. If she ever got her hands on an angel, they were going to get a serious talking-to.

Just breathe.

She dashed forward, hoping the momentum would get her through with less of a fight. Going this way, as it turned out, was much easier. It didn't slow her down at all. She was in the darkness with fireflies, and she could breathe again. The smile on her face was genuine, but the thought of her friends forced her to move quickly. Pain lanced up her side, and she almost crashed to her knees again. It took too long to realize it wasn't her pain; it was coming from somewhere else.

"Where does it hurt?" she said out loud.

Her question was swallowed by the darkness, then part of the darkness glowed red. Betha didn't even think about it—she stepped off of the path in front of her. The red started becoming darker, like blood, and concern washed over her. Somehow, she knew that red was not good in this space of darkness and light. Each time she took a step, her foot created a spark of light like the shining light of the path. The light didn't connect anywhere, but she had faith that she would be okay.

Yet, someone was hurting the paths, stars, and fireflies, and she needed to stop it. The red air trembled, and the pain in her side increased.

"No!"

It was in front of her, the area that was blood red. It stuck out in the night sky, surrounding her. It was like something was trying to poke through the air. Each stab was another jab in her side, but she stayed upright. Once she had figured out the pain wasn't hers, it didn't hurt as much, and she realized she could handle it.

Betha stretched with her power toward the pain in the distance and saw a bright white light in the darkness. The tip of something poked through the spot, and Betha grabbed it with her hand, yanking it toward her. To her shock, a knife came free, flying and tumbling over her shoulder. The pain was still there, but the tear wasn't getting any bigger. Her light covered it, and the red faded along with her pain.

She could finally breathe freely. She realized darkness, fireflies, and stars surrounded her. Somehow, the knife floated in the air. Betha checked over her hand to make sure she wasn't bleeding. The fact that she might have cut herself by grabbing at it hadn't even occurred to her, but her hand was unharmed.

The fireflies danced around the knife and brought it

closer to her. The fireflies swarmed around the knife frantically, but she couldn't understand what they were trying to do. Betha reached out for it, ignoring the fact that her hands were shaking.

As she touched the knife, the fireflies vanished. It was cold, but with her contact, it glowed with her power. "That was a weird hello," she mumbled to herself. The knife itself was around the size of a butter knife. The handle was wrapped in some sort of dark leather, while the blade was clearly made of bone. The tip was pointed but dull.

If this was the knife the demon had been using, then he couldn't open any more tears. They had won. There wouldn't be any more random tears, and that meant they only had to close the ones that already existed.

"We did it!" Betha danced around in a circle, holding the knife in one hand. Laughter bubbled out of her. No big bad guy to fight—she had just stolen the knife when he had tried to use it. It took a moment, but she realized she was off the path. Her feet were on a tiny area that glowed, but it didn't connect to any of the bright doorways that she assumed were portals. She was walking free in this space of night sky and stars, as though she belonged here.

"At least it doesn't hurt anymore." Though as she spoke, she realized she could feel trickles of pain. Older wounds. She focused on these instead of the fact that she had no idea where the door was that would bring her back to Terra. Lost. In some random night sky, surrounded by portals.

"Can you show me the other areas that hurt?" asked

Betha. Fireflies split off from under her feet and retreated into the darkness. She chased them before they got too far ahead. They were a small light in the darkness, and each of her steps glowed as she ran, fading to darkness behind her. This time, the wound was much closer. The tear only had a red tinge around it, but somehow she could tell the knife had caused it.

Betha reached out with her glowing hand and moved to get a closer look. "I wonder where this one goes."

The fireflies landed on the portal, which shimmered like a reflection on a lake. It took a few moments for the image to settle. Betha stepped back in horror. Demons were coming out of the portal in front of her, and she could see the Guard fighting. It was not going well. Bodies lay on the ground— human shaped bodies.

It was unclear where the portal was located. She stepped closer, trying to ignore the fallen. This was on campus—it was the path that led to the volleyball courts. More and more demons flowed out of the portal in a tidal wave. The Guard was struggling, even with bullets flying everywhere.

"I need to heal this. It needs to close." Betha pulled back from the fireflies and focused on the red surrounding the portal. More fireflies joined the ones around the edges of the opening. Betha brought forth her light again and focused on closing the tear.

"Don't worry, I will heal this. It doesn't belong here." Talking to the fireflies helped; they glowed brighter whenever she spoke. Her hands shook as more and more fireflies came out of nowhere. Her hands were covered, then her wrists. Light rose from her center, and she screamed as she could see a familiar Anchor in the distance. That golden hair was in plenty of her dreams, along with his bright blue eyes.

ANGIE SUDDENLY SMILED, and the surrounding troops looked surprised. She wasn't one to smile about anything. "We will push them back tonight and hold this ground. We will NOT lose the college. St. Luna is ours!" Everyone looked at her, startled. Minutes ago, they had been talking about the best way to retreat and where they should hold the line.

"Betha is back! She's coming!" Angie motioned toward the tear in the distance. She could feel her Traveler there, but it made little sense. It was as if she was flickering in and out of existence.

"Betha?" asked Angie through their bond.

Without waiting for a response, Angie headed outside of the chapel. If the fates were willing, they could do this. They would hold this ground, and reinforcements were on the way. Betha would show up with a host of angels. It didn't matter that she had told herself the same thing every day for the last week. It would be today. It had to be. They would hold back the tide coming from the portal.

Who knew that when they had stopped that demon from opening a tear on campus that this was what waited on the other side? The school wouldn't have survived this then, and now they had to hold the line or retreat. With Betha here, they would hold the line.

Something flickered on the edge of her awareness. Her focus went to the tear. "Betha?" A Guard member nudged her to get her back in the game. She blinked, then glanced around at the troops with a smile. "We need to hold the tide! The Traveler is here!" Her voice rose in a howl even though she kept her human form as Betha flickered back and forth in her mind.

"The tear is glowing!" yelled someone closer to the fighting. Soldiers that were around the makeshift headquarters grabbed their weapons and headed toward the battle line to join the men already fighting.

"We need to help her!" Angie yelled. She shifted and charged toward the battlefield, roaring an attack howl. Other shifters joined her call. It echoed all across campus, the news spreading like wildfire. Her paws ate up the ground, but she needed to move quicker. The tear loomed in the distance. She was going to help Betha close it again. This time for good.

"I'm coming, Betha!" yelled Angie through their link.

~

ERIC AND CARTER were on the front lines fighting for the school as Angie shouted in their heads.

"Angie?" Carter moved forward, closer to the tear as it glowed. He could feel Betha for the first time in ages. He had left James at the Nexus, who had promised to guard it with his life.

"Eric! It's Betha—we need to move!" Carter moved toward the tear instead of holding the line. With each shot, another demon stumbled. Eric's wings flared out behind him as he struck where he could with his sword, angel fire glowing in the light. Even though demons were still traveling through the portal, it was smaller. Suddenly three feet on either side of the giant hole had closed. It cut some demons in half. The stampede slowed, and demons tumbled about in confusion. That was all the Guard needed, and they gained ground.

A dark shadow darted near Carter—Angie stuck near him as they made their way closer to the tear. There was power in a pack, even one as mixed as theirs. Each demon that died was not being replaced anymore, and the gunfire increased. Determination rang in the air. The Guard moved with focus; each step forward was more ground. They were going to win on this day. The tear was closing, and they all fought harder as the demon numbers shrank.

The tear shimmered, and Carter swore he saw Betha standing there, bright light streaming from her hands to the edges. "*Betha!*" he called.

The black blur moved faster, darting between demons and clearing the path, along with other shifters on four paws. Carter ran toward Betha, watching the edges of the portal. All they needed was for a demon to turn around and see the Traveler instead of the hell they'd come from. They could attack her. The light coming from the tear increased, and it shone like the sunrise on a cloudless morning.

Carter kept firing as Betha stepped forward, the tear closing behind her. Demons stood between them. Shifters surged forward, tackling whomever they could. Cheers started up from somewhere behind Carter, and the gunfire slowed. He locked eyes with Betha. She was glowing, and fireflies darted around her before fading from sight.

The exhaustion was plain on her face as he rushed toward her, dropping his gun. Her body swayed, and he didn't want her to hit the blood-soaked ground. Carter needed to touch her and feel that she was real, that this wasn't a dream. He had just caught her as lightning rushed into his body. His scream tore through the air as pain raced up and down his spine until he blacked out.

CHAPTER
THIRTY-TWO

Betha did not know what had happened. One moment she was healing the tear, then she was on the battlefield, and Angie was yanking Carter out of her arms. Eric had taken Carter, and now Angie was carrying her. Church bells rang in the distance, and everything was muffled.

Angie set her down and put a cup of water in her hands. Betha quickly slammed it when she realized how thirsty she was. A sandwich followed the water, and she scarfed it down like no tomorrow. Things became more than blurs and unrecognizable words.

"Betha, are you okay?" asked her best friend. Angie sat next to her, and Betha focused on her until everything became clear. A healer hovered nearby, reaching out with healing power, but they didn't touch her. The healer gave a nod to Angie before leaving the room.

"I think so. The fireflies led me to the tear after I stepped off the path. I am pretty sure that I closed it. Right?" The darkness and the stars flashed through her mind, along with the fact that she had picked up the knife. She could feel the weight of it in her vest pocket.

"Yes, you did. What happened?" Angie's voice was nice and soft, like she was doing her best to remain calm. It took a moment for Betha to realize that quite a few people surrounded her. Several she did not know, though she recognized Justin, the Alpha from Angie's Pack.

"I got to the angelic world, but no one was there. It was empty, with no one guarding their gate. No one at the midpoint. The air and light are wrong there. I couldn't breathe. I had to leave." Her voice sounded so loud. "Then something tried to create a tear. I stopped it, then was led to this tear and saw the demons coming through."

Angie shook her head at Eric, but he stepped forward anyway and said, "I think she meant, what did you do to Carter?"

Betha thought about it. She had stepped out of the portal, and Carter had caught her. Then a rush of power, and Carter screamed. It sounded like the one from before, from when he was dying.

"Where's Carter?" Betha jumped to her feet in sudden panic, looking around the room at everyone. Angie and Eric quickly cleared the room, looking worried. "What happened?" Betha demanded.

"My brother is recovering. He is going to be okay." Eric reached out to embrace her, and Angie tried to stop him, but Betha grabbed his hand. She didn't miss Angie flinching at the contact. Eric wrapped his arm around her shoulders, and she could feel his sincerity. "It's all right."

"Recovering from what?" asked Betha quietly. She had done something. A second time, she had done something to Carter without asking.

"Manifesting," said Eric.

"Wait, what?" Betha exclaimed. She looked between the two of them as they led her down the hallway to the healing quarters. Carter lay on his belly, his vest cut off of him, with bright white wings jutting out from his back.

"What the fuck?" whispered Betha. This didn't happen. People usually manifested in their teens, if not sooner. The early twenties were super rare. The late twenties, never.

"Yeah, that's what we were thinking," Angie said.

Betha stood there with her mouth open before closing it slowly.

Eric moved forward and took his brother's hand, tears in his eyes. "He's okay, just out cold from the physical shock of manifesting. It has never happened this late to someone angelic. When he caught you, that light..."

Betha grabbed a chair and sat down near the bed. How could she have caused this, of all things? "I don't know. I passed out in the angelic realm. Like I said, it was weird there." She shook her head. "I don't want to go back anytime soon."

Betha switched to mind-speak. *"I found the knife."*

Eric's eyes went wide, but he kept his mouth shut as the door was open.

Angie gave her a giant grin. "Betha, eight points. Demon, three," she said out loud. Betha was curious as to how Angie was keeping track of the score. *"We wondered what happened—tears stopped opening two weeks ago,*" replied Angie in her head.

"Only three portals opened? In two weeks?" Betha asked.

Angie motioned for Betha to get up to leave the room. "You should shower, and I will catch you up. Eric can hang here with Carter until you are rested."

Betha moved forward and squeezed Carter's hand before following Angie. She glanced back at the twins. Eric looked down at his brother with such joy on his face. She knew this moment would be a treasured memory for a long time.

~

ANGIE DID NOT WANT to have this conversation with Betha, but Eric and Carter had nominated her before Betha had even come back. It was up to her, and she was thankful that Betha had asked no more questions. Or commented on the two-week remark. Hearing Betha's voice inside her head was amazing, and she had missed it so much. Even though Betha's journey sounded crazy, and she needed to hear more details eventually, now it was time to discuss what had happened on their end while Betha was gone.

The clock ticked so slowly as Betha showered. Angie did her best to relax, but she paced until her friend shut the shower off. Then Angie sat down on the couch and tried to remain calm.

Betha opened the bathroom door and gave a sad

smile. “So, I know it must be bad. I could feel your footsteps and your anxiety. Let me get dressed first.”

Angie tried to say something, hesitated, then took a deep breath. “I drew the short straw to debrief you.”

“Okay, that is ominous.”

Angie nodded and waited to start until Betha finished putting on some clean clothes. “It isn’t great—I was hoping you could sleep before we talked, but I figured our emotions would keep you up. It’s bad, Betha. You were gone for just over thirty-two days. Longer than any of us thought you would be.”

Angie watched the puzzlement cross her friend’s face before she added in a rush, “That’s not the worst. They figured out who you are. The demons attacked Luna’s Grace. Your mom was taken.”

~

Betha flinched, and she could feel the bile rising in her throat. She dashed toward the bathroom, barely making it to the toilet before bringing up the sandwich she had eaten earlier. Tears rolled down her face, and it was like she was losing her mother all over again.

“Shh. It will be okay.” Angie held her hair and rubbed her back.

“He has my mom?” The silence was all the confirmation that she needed. This was just too much. It took too long to get herself under control and stop heaving. “Why would he want my mom? When did this happen?”

Angie handed over a washcloth and a glass of water. “Literally a day after you stepped through the portal, the attack happened. It has been pure chaos since. Add in that we thought you would be back within two weeks, and things became rather bleak after the fourteen-day mark. When additional tears stopped opening, we rallied, but folks were losing hope."

Betha slowly climbed to her feet and tried not to let anger take over. She had left, and her family had suffered.

"That's not all," continued Angie. "The staff at Luna's Grace found a journal your mother left behind for you. The council wanted to take it but agreed to have me read it in case there was something inside that would help us." Angie pulled out a book from under her pillow. "It is mostly a scrapbook of your early years, but she wrote some notes to you. I think you should read it. I didn't understand most of it, but it might mean something different to you."

Betha took the journal from Angie with shaky hands. "What is he going to do with my mom? He snagged her before I stopped him from making any more tears."

Angie's voice was soft as she replied, "Kyra thinks he might try to create another one."

"Oh, fates," whispered Betha. Tears trailed down her face. Her mother was in the hands of a demon, and she had no way to protect herself. The last time she had seen Josephine, it was touch and go even understanding who people were.

"Yeah, like I said, it's bad."

CHAPTER THIRTY-THREE

Betha was hiding, or trying to, in the healers' wing. The scrapbook that Angie had given her was tucked in her shoulder bag. She hadn't been able to open it. Instead, she was in Carter's room. He hadn't awoken yet, though the healers said it should be any time now. Angie and Eric both knew where she was but hadn't commented on it.

This was the second time she had violated Carter's consent. First, she had made him an Anchor, and now she had forced a manifestation on him. Eric had reassured her that Carter was going to be okay with this, but until she heard it from his own mouth, she was going to be uneasy.

"Hey Betha, I heard you might be in here," said Joey from the doorway. He gave her a goofy grin as he approached. "Still can't believe that is possible," he said, gesturing to Carter.

"You aren't the only one," said Betha.

"How about we take a short walk?" he asked. "I am

not a fan of this wing, for obvious reasons." Betha remembered his foot being crushed in the attack on campus. So much had happened since then, but at the same time, it wasn't that long ago.

Betha stood up, grabbing her bag. "Are you sure you should be walking around this much?"

Joey waited until they were in the hall. "My foot will be fine. I am working on flexibility in PT. I only lost a toe. Eric pulled together enough of the bone that the rest was saved. I should have a cane, but I keep forgetting it everywhere. Heck, the toe might even grow back over time, they aren't sure."

"I didn't realize Eric was such a powerful healer," said Betha. She walked slowly, watching Joey walk beside her. He was doing pretty well, but she noticed that his gait was weird.

Joey shrugged. "Yeah, I guess if he focused on it, he could be one of the best. I overheard one of the healers mention it was such a waste of talent. I owe him one."

Betha spotted an open bench in the courtyard and headed in that direction. "You don't owe him anything. Eric is Eric. Do you know where Ben got sent to?"

The two sat together. They had a great view of all of the people dashing about. The healer wing was busier than one would hope, with all the attacks the past few weeks. At least the attacks had finally decreased. Most of the injured on campus were shifters, and they bounced back quickly from pretty much anything that wasn't fatal.

"Poor guy, he is with a unit in the city. His tech skills are being put to good use, but messages are few and far between." Joey rolled his eyes and deadpanned, "I think he found a girl in his unit he is interested in, so you lost your chance with him."

Betha couldn't stop the laughter from rolling out of her. Joey's delivery had been perfect, and her laughter was contagious. He was soon laughing right along with her. Maybe everything would work out all right after all. Laughter was, as her mother used to whisper to her, the best medicine.

THE MOONLIGHT SHONE down on her in the darkness. Betha knew she was asleep, or at least her body was. She was less and less sure that this place was only a dream. Here, she thought about the book her mother had left her, the book she had just gone through.

Someday you will be able to return home. You have so many family members waiting to meet you. Learn, grow, and trust your Anchors.

The notes Betha's mother had left her hidden in the journal helped make sense of why she had made the choices she had. Other parts she didn't understand, and a good chunk of it was a scrapbook. There were only small mentions of her father in the book, but nothing that would lead to his identity. Only that he knew Josephine was going to leave him, and that he understood why.

The scrapbook contained everything from fragments of sentences to directions that made little sense, and even tiny sketches. A star on the page usually meant that there was a note hidden somewhere that she needed to read. It had taken time to go page by page, and she had kept her own notes from what she read. Sometimes the hidden note she had found was only that her mother loved her.

Our seer foretold your birth. She knew Terra would need you. I willingly gave up everything so you would be you. It was worth it. You were worth it. I am sorry to leave you this burden, but I know you will succeed. Whatever happens, remember that Travelers are protectors of the space in-between. We are sworn to protect it, and it protects the heart of hearts. You were born in-between and can walk the darkest paths.

Betha needed to talk to Kyra about the pathways that she had walked when she had traveled between the portals. Closing her eyes for a moment, she was grateful that she had this space, whether it was a dream or not. At least once a week, she ended up here when she went to bed. Waking up always left her refreshed and ready to tackle the day. Her mind drifted to the fact that she was here, and that her mother had put her on this path. Her trust in her mother was rocky, but her mother always wanted the best for her. She felt more centered than ever. They would get her mother back and close the remaining tears. The Guard was gaining ground with securing two of the remaining tears, so they were making progress even while she and her team recovered.

Closing the tear on campus and reappearing had inspired everyone. Motivation and planning were the current focus while new tears weren't being opened. She was glad that she didn't have to figure all of that out. All she needed to concentrate on was the tears, the pathways, and her mother. What happened to Carter was a mystery, but it hopefully was a one-off, and it wouldn't happen again. After all, none of her other Anchors were un-manifested, so maybe it couldn't happen again.

Betha was trying to be patient for him to wake up, but he was undergoing changes, and that took time. The speed at which he grew wings freaked out the whole healer house, and if the council hadn't been meeting, he would have been surrounded by the members.

She opened her eyes slowly in her private place to gaze up at the moon, and her thoughts drifted to the fireflies. Betha had asked her Anchors if they had seen them. They had, but no one else on the battlefield had. It was strange and must be an Anchor thing, though she was getting sick of lumping everything unexplained into that category. The space between the portals—the pathways—had spoken to her like the fireflies in her dreams. Betha was pretty sure that they were the in-between that her mother mentioned in her journal. It made sense to her, and the more she listened to her gut, the more things seemed to work out. A firefly drifted in front of her face, and she couldn't help but smile and try to boop it with one finger.

The "heart of hearts" was still a mystery, but it wasn't urgent to figure that out. While getting a business degree and saving money to open up a café had been her dream for as long as she could remember, that had to be set aside now. This was what she was meant to do; it was like a key fit into place inside her heart. Turning away from that old, comfortable dream wasn't as hard as she had thought it was going to be. Plus, she could always do that when all of this was over with.

Fireflies danced to music that she couldn't hear, and happiness spread over her. For a moment, she swore she could smell her mother's perfume. Tears formed in the corners of her eyes, but she wiped them away. "I don't know if I can save you, Mom, but I love you so much." The fireflies gathered closer to her, humming in the night sky, the music flickering in and out.

"I am a Traveler, and I will protect the leylines."

Her voice broke on the last word, but she meant it even as she let the tears roll down her face.

Justin looked around the table at the various representatives. Hopefully, this was going to be a more cheerful meeting. The last couple of weeks had been counts of dead, stats on how likely they were to be able to stop the demons, and increasing the draft.

The head of the council called the meeting to order, and Justin noted Kyra was in the room.

"As most of you are aware, yesterday Traveler Betha arrived back on Earth at the St. Luna tear, closing it. During the crossing, she touched Anchor Carter, causing a late onset of his manifestation." Muttering around the table grew, and most turned to look at Kellion.

Kellion gave a nod to the council head before speaking. "It is true. Carter has manifested."

The muttering increased, and someone spoke up,

"How the heck did that happen? He was human; we all know it."

Kellion raised a hand to quiet the group. "We believe she brought back angelic power from that world and it jump-started Carter's dormant genes. It was tested on other individuals, but there wasn't a reaction for them. It was a one-time occurrence, and it manifested her Anchor."

He motioned toward Kyra, who took over the conversation. "The Traveler also brought word that she had destroyed the magic that the demon was using to create tears."

Several people smiled, though some were still stuck on the fact that the Traveler had caused a human to manifest. Justin wished he had been there to see it, though he had walked past the room Carter was staying in. The guy had wings, and he didn't used to.

"We believe we need to gain control of the rest of the tears and close them. The Traveler and Anchors are dealing with the tear forty minutes west as we speak. From there, they will take care of the one in the city. The numbers should only decrease from here on out. The bad news is that it sounded like the heavens have been put into lockdown. Traveler Betha could not contact any of the angels. We assume this is why our request for aid went unanswered. Still, with the magic used to open the tears destroyed, we should be able to take care of this mess ourselves."

As Justin looked around the room, his eyes landed on Andrea, who wasn't smiling, but she did not speak up. The council head brought order back to the meeting, discussing plans to take out the remaining tear down south.

Kellion looked concerned and motioned to speak. "We need to figure out why the heavens are on lockdown. The only time that has happened in my memory is during—" Alarms sounded, causing several members to jump up. "—the war," mumbled Kellion.

Kyra headed for the door. "If you want to stay in here, I will close the portal and formalize a complete lockdown. Otherwise you have ten seconds!"

Justin jumped to his feet. He quickly darted outside with several council members, though a few remained inside, per protocol. They couldn't let anything happen to the entire council at once. Kellion joined him in the hall and, to his surprise, James was in the hallway yelling about demons. The council lands were under attack, yet he couldn't figure out why. They would need a magical army to do any actual damage.

Kellion, Justin, and James moved slowly through the halls, clearing any demons they came across. It was too easy. Angel fire flickered down the hallway. Kyra took up the rear guard. James' cellphone went off, but he ignored it as they cleared the courtyard near the Nexus. The Guards were holding chokepoints, and Kellion could wipe out whole groups with his angel fire. Strategy was on their side. The whole complex was built that way. This attack made little sense.

"James, where is Betha?" asked Kyra.

He looked back at her blankly, and amidst the battle, a sense of sudden anxiety washed over them all.

CHAPTER THIRTY-FOUR

Betha couldn't believe that Eric was giving dating advice to Angie about Joey. She knew he was doing it to distract her from worrying, and it was working. Everyone was a little off since Carter wasn't with them. Add in that Jessica wasn't there either, and the team felt a little vulnerable. They still had Brutis, but everyone could feel the gap. Unfortunately, they came to the checkpoint, and Eric parked the car, ending the distracting dating advice. It didn't take long for them to get ready to head into the field, mostly in silence.

One of the head Guards approached to give them an update. "Things are calm this morning. Only a few groups have crossed here, and we are holding down the fort. It's unusual. We have called it in, but all three locations seem to be quiet this morning."

The group looked at each other.

Eric nodded at Betha. "How about we get this one closed fast, then get back to the city?"

Everyone agreed, and they headed down the clearing

to the tear. Most demons that crossed did everything they could to fight their way outside of the Guard and then flee into the world. Some bigger groups just came across to attack, then would jump back through the tear after doing damage. The fact that it was quiet was unsettling. Something was going on—either this was a trap, or somewhere else was going up in flames, somewhere they didn't know about.

Betha had a sword this time as her main weapon, while she had a rifle as a backup. It was getting easier for her to call up angel fire in small bursts. After returning to Terra yesterday, it would come on command, but only for short lengths of time. Awareness flickered, and she froze. "A group is crossing," she whispered. The Guards who had gone on ahead started fighting, and Betha's group waited until the all-clear was given. They made it to the edge of the tear with no issues. Everyone took up a formation to guard Betha as she began the work to close it.

The closing itself was easy, then the Guard started cheering. It didn't take long for everyone to make it back to the car. The Guards were packing up, and a light Guard crew to man the location was being set up. Eric went off to go talk to the Guard chief while Brutis stuck close to Betha and Angie. Both stayed in animal form.

"This doesn't feel right," said Betha.

"*It doesn't. What are we missing?*" asked Angie.

"I don't know, but I think we should get back."

Eric headed returned. "They are going to keep extra folks here and clear out slower. I have the feeling we need to get back to the city."

Within moments, they were back in the car. Angie stayed in wolf form while Brutis changed back since he didn't fit in the car in his larger panther form. He had grabbed a rifle out of the back just in case. The tension was thick, and everyone stayed quiet on the drive.

"Okay, does everyone else feel this tension?" Betha broke the silence.

Eric drove faster than normal while she tried to call Grandpappy on speaker phone.

Angie's window was down, and her wolf head stuck out. Betha was pretty sure Angie was the only one enjoying the moment. *"I can have fun even though things feel screwed up."*

That got a smirk out of Betha at least.

Eric spoke up, "No, the feeling that we need to get back to the city has increased twofold. I think it might be leaking into our link, which is why all of us feel it." The car sped up a bit more, and her phone went to voicemail. Grandpappy's voice launched into how you could leave a message, but he wouldn't get back to you.

Brutis turned toward Betha from the passenger seat. "I am not in the family, so to speak, and even I feel uncertain. That tear closing was too simple. Where did all the demons go?"

"We are only thirty minutes out." Eric's phone rang through the car's speakers, and Susan's name popped up on the screen. He hit the answer button and said. "Now isn't—"

"Stop the car!" Susan shouted.

Eric slammed on the brakes immediately, and Angie hit the seat in front of her hard, her head still out the window. A yelp sounded from the wolf. Everyone else, thankfully, had seat belts on.

Susan continued, "The council lands are under attack. It's a trap—he is waiting for you on the road ahead!"

"Who's waiting?" asked Eric.

"The demon, the head one who was opening tears, he's waiting for Betha. That's all I saw. I need to go!" The click of her hanging up was sudden, and everyone in the car looked at Eric, trying to figure out what just happened.

"Was that Susan from my economics class, Susan?" asked Betha.

Eric's hands tightened on the steering wheel. "She can see things. Fuck!" He slammed his fists down. Worry for his brother flooded into the bond. "I need to think," he muttered.

Betha looked over at Angie, who was trying to climb out of the gap in between the seats and said, "Angie and Brutis should go out on foot. We will keep going in the car. We can turn it from a trap into an ambush."

"It's as good a plan as any," said Brutis.

Eric took a deep breath, but Betha was already out of the car, opening Angie's door. "We will stay in touch, and Angie can keep us in the loop." Angie scrambled to the ground as Brutis got out of the car before he shifted.

"*I can sneak forward and scout things out,*" sent Angie.

Eric released his grip on the steering wheel and looked out the door at the shifters. "Be careful out there."

Waiting for Brutis to shift again seemed to take forever, but then the two shifters headed off into the woods. Betha climbed into the passenger seat and couldn't help but think it only took a trap to get her into the front seat. Up until now, she had been relegated to the back seat.

"I hope Carter is okay, though the school should be safe if it's the council lands that are under attack." Betha poked her mind out toward Carter, but he hadn't moved yet on her radar.

"So far, no signs of anything out of the ordinary. I would drive at a normal speed. Turns out Brutis can be fast when needed," added Angie.

Eric put the car into drive and started forward. "Here we go. We should have known this was coming. Are you ready, Betha?"

She took a deep breath before replying. "I think so."

"Don't do anything that Carter wouldn't do. I don't think he would forgive me if anything happened to you."

Betha just shook her head. "I mean, that's one way to show you care." He had to do a double take to realize that she was poking fun at him.

"You know I care, but Carter is like your big brother or uncle. I don't know how our relationship works yet. I mean, I am an Anchor, but besides that, yeah, I don't know," Eric finished awkwardly.

Talk about a direct blow across her heart, but Betha ignored it.

"We haven't had a ton of time to spend together. I have been training with Carter as much as possible. Angie, I have known forever, and, well, you have been fighting demons nonstop. We will figure it all out once this is taken care of," said Betha. Her thoughts went to her mother and what lay ahead on the road. Focusing on her breathing helped.

"*We smell demons up ahead, more than I would like given that there are only us four. We're going to circle around. I am going to pick off any of them that I can one by one once you both arrive. Maybe call in backup from the camp we just left?*" sent Angie.

Betha could feel the worry coming from Angie, which was unusual for her. "Thoughts? Should we call for backup?"

"Angie can be a one-woman army in the darkness, but with this sunlight, it'll be harder." Eric called the camp they had just left and spoke for a few moments before hanging up. "They're already heading this way. They heard about the attack. They are maybe five to ten minutes behind us. We only need to stall for that long."

His voice trailed off as they came around the bend. In the middle of the road stood a figure dressed in black. He almost looked human, but his eyes were glowing as he held a knife against Josephine's throat.

CHAPTER THIRTY-FIVE

Angie started her killing spree at the point farthest away from the car that she could see. Brutis stayed in a tree near the road, ready to provide backup to Eric and Betha. Demons were hiding in the forest, but they had spaced themselves out. Thankfully, she had shadows to work with and could port from tree to tree. The sun wasn't completely overhead, and each tree cast some darkness that gave her room.

The plan was simple—each one hiding behind a tree in shadow, she would grab and yank to the shadow plane. From there, killing them was easy. Complete darkness made it hard to fight her since she was invisible there. The number of demons waiting for an ambush was daunting. It was clear where all the creatures had been gathering from the tear they had just closed.

While her plan was sound, she really hoped that Eric had called for backup. Angie could feel Betha slowly getting closer, so she moved quicker. This was what she had trained for and why her species had been hunted down. Now she was the last one left. Something that could move from shadow to shadow, and bring someone with them, was dangerous.

Dragging the first into the shadows without a scream was easy. One moment was all she needed and then they were on her turf.

Bit by bit, she worked her way back toward the car that had now stopped in the middle of the road. Angie couldn't see it because of the trees, but Betha had stopped moving inside her head. Time was passing, and the shadows were getting a bit smaller. Five down, way too many to go.

The emotions coming from Betha were intense, but Angie did her best to ignore them. Each demon disposed of was one that wouldn't hurt her family. The closer she got, the more she noticed something odd in the wind.

"*There are demons surrounding the car!*" sent Angie in panic.

She could smell Brutis on the wind, but there wasn't a way to warn him. Angie quickly moved in that direction, hoping she would get there in time to help.

~

Betha stared straight out the windshield at the demon that held her mother. For a moment, everything inside her wanted to scream, then she took a breath and did her best to relax her fists. She slowly opened the door and held her hands out to show that they were empty. As she stepped around the door, she caught her mother's eyes. The fact that her mother was still alive was such a relief. In the back of her mind, she had worried that it was already too late.

"You need to let her go," said Betha, a deadly calm in her voice.

She could hear Eric open his door, but the demon jerked the knife.

"He gets to stay in the car," growled the demon.

Betha glanced back at Eric and shook her head. Angie's voice rang out that demons were circling around the back of the car, and it took everything for her to not look around.

"Let my mother go," Betha repeated to the demon standing in the road.

The smile that came over the demon's face was disturbing. His mouth was too big for his face and eat tooth was pointed. "That is no way to speak to a prince," said the demon in front of her. His blue and red eyes pulsed in the daylight. "If you give me the knife, I will give her to you."

Betha nodded frantically. "You can give my mother to Eric, and I will give you the knife."

"What are you doing?" asked Eric silently.

"Eric, trust me. We need you out of that car," answered Betha in turn.

The demon glared at her but motioned for Eric to get out of the car.

"I can see a demon on either side of the road. An upper-class demon like the one with your mother," sent Eric.

Betha could only just hear Eric's door opening over

the thudding of her heart. Her eyes caught her mother's again, then her mother smiled. Betha could see that her mom recognized her. It wasn't always the case, and it could change suddenly.

"Mom, don't worry—you will be fine soon." Betha started to step toward the demon but froze as the demon Eric had warned her about stepped out of the trees. He looked like the one holding her mother, but he had armor on, along with a sword. Oh fuck.

"You will give the knife to my lieutenant, then I will give your mother to your friend," said the prince. Despite the shiny armor, Betha didn't let her gaze drop from the one who was clearly in charge.

"Betha, don't!" Her mother's voice rang out as she struggled with the demon, trying to jerk out of his hold. It was like a signal had gone off, and she heard Brutis roar. A black blur flew from the trees and tackled the armored demon while Betha darted for her mom.

Light flared from her left side, and she assumed Eric had brought forth his angel fire. The demon struggled to hold onto her mother, who kicked at his knee. Everything slowed as he slid the sharp knife across her throat.

"Mom!"

BETHA KEPT RUNNING FORWARD as the demon prince dropped her mother to the ground and grinned. Blood spilled across the pavement. It was so red, like the wound in the in-between.

"Mother!"

"That's right, Traveler, come right to me. Time to take you home." The demon gave her a wide, toothy grin, and he motioned for her to come closer. "You will earn me my throne." He still held the dagger covered in her mother's blood. Anger rose up in Betha, and white lights blossomed at the mark on her wrist.

"What? No!" Fear covered the prince's face for the first time as he stepped back. Betha wasn't sure what he saw, only that she could tell he was not prepared. She didn't feel like a weak girl anymore. She was a Traveler, and she knew what to do.

Betha would have sworn she felt Carter there, guiding her hands. Inside her head, she could feel a bright white light. She darted forward, drawing the knife and thrusting it at the demon, directly into the center of his chest. Her speed and accuracy were beyond anything she had been able to manage before, and as she stabbed, time slowed. Her hand moved as if Carter were wielding it, blocking a clumsy slash from the demon. When she'd made contact, that bright light inside her head had connected. White angel fire flowed down her hand and jumped down the blade, igniting the demon's chest. Time sped up again.

The demon screamed as white fire flicked over his form. Betha took a small step back and tripped to the ground. Gunshots came from behind her, but her mother was on the pavement.

"Mom!" Betha got next to her on her hands and knees. "Mom, it will be okay. You will be okay. Eric!" She tried to stop the bleeding, but it wasn't working. Blood covered her hands. "Eric!" Tears dripped down her face as she realized that her mother wasn't responding. Her eyes were open but no longer looked at her.

"No no no no. Mom, I love you. Don't go."

Then Angie was there, pulling her off the ground and into her arms. Betha couldn't help it as the grief took over, pouring out of her in great, racking sobs.

CHAPTER THIRTY-SIX

The plan hadn't worked. The council members had fought back, and it had kept the angel Kellion distracted, but it had been like tossing soldiers into a meat grinder. Most of the prince's forces had been slaughtered at the Nexus. The death toll had been high, and it dismayed the butler that they had lost so many, especially so pointlessly. The whole thing had been unsuccessful from the beginning. He wished he could have changed the prince's mind, but so it was with the noble houses. You had to listen to orders.

After the prince had gone up in angel fire, the trusted butler quickly fled along with one other lieutenant that hadn't gone crazy over his liege's death. The breaking of the bond the prince had over his inferiors had rippled across all of the demons he had commanded. They all knew he was gone. A new hierarchy needed to be figured out as soon as possible. The trip back to the city was short, and dodging Guards had become second nature to them. The butler crossed the tear as quickly as he could during the upheaval; he needed to go report to the regent what had happened.

The price was dead, the knife was gone, and Terra was a mess. This could either go badly or very well. Once they were back in hell, it was quick to travel to the castle where the regent was currently holding court. The lieutenant fast-traveled them across the desolate world; it was one of his gifts. They landed in the receiving room where servants bustled about. The butler looked around at all the activity, and he couldn't help but wonder what was going on. The last time that they had checked in with the family, the king was still leading the war against the angels, and the princess was sitting on the throne as regent.

The demons on either side of the door to the throne room gave nods to the lieutenant and opened the door.

THE PRINCESS SAT with one leg thrown over the armrest, her black armor polished. Red light spilled from the crown on her head. It was good to be the favored child. Yet, as her eyes traveled to the butler walking around the throne room, she wanted to frown. The tall lieutenant next to the butler created a warm feeling inside of her. Her brother's keepers were here. How interesting.

When he was the correct distance away, the butler went down to one knee and waited for permission to get up. Finally she waved her hand, and he climbed to his feet. He was slower than she remembered getting up from the floor. The butler had taken care of both her and her brother, the prince. He was the only demon she had voiced her concerns to about her brother's instability during their childhood. She learned quickly how to do what she was told and follow in the king's footsteps. It had paid off. Now she was regent. Only one of them could rule after the king was gone. Each day that went by, she was closer to her goal.

"So, what trouble has my darling brother gotten into now? Your last report was rather lacking. His lands are rather empty at the moment, and all the lesser shock troops are scattered."

"Your Highness, the prince is dead," replied the old servant.

The princess sat up straight, and her eyes narrowed. "He got himself killed?" Her gaze turned to the lieutenant next to him, who nodded. "Well, that makes things much easier; I won't need to deal with him now. Or his constant, if not inept, backstabbing." She shook her head, sending her curls all over the place, though the crown stayed in place. With a hand, she motioned to an attendant near the wall. "Start reorganizing whatever men he has left. We will take control of his lands and add them to our personal holdings. Draft a letter to the king—I will want to read it before it goes out."

It was clear to the butler that he was dismissed, but he stayed in his place. Within a few moments, her gaze turned back toward him. "Yes?" Her eyes narrowed again, and she let her annoyance at his continued presence show.

"There were some complications, for your ears only."

He quickly bowed his head seeking forgiveness and held that position, keeping his eyes on the floor.

The princess motioned, and everyone cleared the room. She darted forward and used a finger to lift his chin back up. Her voice soft, she asked, "What did my truly idiotic sibling do?"

"He took the knife, Princess. A Traveler now has it." His voice broke as he mentioned the new Traveler, and that the prince had attacked the council. He also quickly recapped the message that he had sent the king about how the prince was losing his sanity.

Anger rose inside her at the mention of the knife being taken. How had he been so stupid? "I will need to report this personally to the king. I had received a letter asking to send it to the front lines and to take care of my brother."

At least she didn't need to kill him now. Yet the knife was gone. This was going to complicate everything with the king. He didn't take failure well. Finally, she nodded. "It is the height of stupidity, but still believable that my brother stole the knife from the armory and snuck some demons over to Earth to have some fun. He did not survive the encounter and lost the knife to the Travelers. If he had survived, I'd have skinned him, then killed him anyway. Pity."

The butler quickly nodded his head at the revised story. "Yes, Your Highness, he became very unstable."

The princess walked away from him, and she heard a sigh of relief. Then his head was tumbling free to the ground. "It is too bad that you didn't escape with *your* life." The sword in her was dripping.

She didn't let emotion show on her face, but it had been a kinder death than what the king would have done. The body smoked, then burned, while the head stayed where it was on the stone floor.

"It can be so hard to find good help."

THE CROWD around the pyre surprised Betha. When her mother had started showing signs of memory loss, there had only been a few hands to help her. Yet the people surrounding the area showed how many were going to miss her. She spotted her mother's nurse from Luna's Grace, Angie's parents, and plenty of her mother's older friends. Then there was the group that was there for *her*. All of her Anchors, and happily, Joey was by Angie's side.

Grandpappy was appraising Joey when he noticed she had joined the group. He gave her a soft smile but stayed near Kyra.

Carter moved through the crowd and pulled her into a hug. "Are you ready for this?" he asked gently. Betha took a deep breath of his scent—pine needles and gunpowder. It hadn't been clear if he was going to be able to attend. His wings were folded against his back since he wasn't able to vanish them yet.

"As much as I can be," whispered Betha.

He gave her another squeeze before pulling away and taking her hand. The thudding of her heart and confusion of emotions was almost too much to handle. Kyra caught her eye, and Betha nodded for the elder Traveler to start. She had been surprised when Kyra had asked to say the ritual goodbye for her mother. It had something to do with Traveler tradition.

Kyra cleared her throat and then said, "We are here today to say goodbye to Josephine. She was a wayward Traveler who chose Terra as her home. Her greatest joy in life was being a mother, and she gave all that she was to protect her daughter.

"We bid farewell to Josephine, as she now journeys to the heart of the worlds, and the fates call her home. May your light shine as you now take your final journey among the in-between, dear sister. We will miss you."

Kyra nodded, and James set a red stone on the pyre. Flame leaped up rapidly, consuming the wood and cloth. Betha held her tears at bay but squeezed Carter's hand tighter. The heat from the fire was offset by the coldness of the blade hidden under her jacket.

Betha had never been so ready to crawl into bed before. Her mother's death was only one death among so many. The feeling of being completely tired dragged down her limbs. Closing the city tears had been a piece of cake, and they only had one more to go, far to the south. It seemed with the death of the ringleader, demons were fleeing back through the tears or out to the forest. Guards were taking care of any that were causing problems, and that would continue for some time yet. That wasn't her problem though.

So many had died, and for what? Just because of a demon who had started trouble. They had captured one of the upper-class demons after the ringleader had gone down. The council was getting as much information as they could. This was not an attack by the king of hell, only his outcast son. That one person could cause so much death and destruction was horrid.

The moon wasn't full above her this time, in her special place. Instead, it was a crescent moon. The fireflies were subdued as they danced about her, reading her somber mood. She pulled the knife out of her inside vest pocket. It was going everywhere with her these days, though she hadn't known if it would show up here as well. In the moonlight, it glowed, and it warmed in her hands. Without the knife, the prince wouldn't have been able to cause all of this. Betha let her tears fall. The fireflies danced around the glowing knife. They didn't seem to think it was evil. But all she wanted to do was to destroy it.

"I protected the leylines, yet we still lost." Her mind drifted to her mother lying on the pavement, eyes unseeing. "I still lost her." The fact that she had lost a big part of her mother when she had gone to Luna's Grace wasn't discounted. This time, though, it was final, and any hope that her mother would get better was gone.

The smell of her mother's perfume crossed her face, and she flinched as hands cupped hers. Betha's head snapped upward. Her mother kneeled there, glowing in the moonlight. The fireflies danced around her, steadying her mother's light. "You didn't lose me. I will always be with you." Josephine reached up and cupped her face, wiping away a tear. The warmth from her mother's palm was real. "This needed to happen, and you need to learn to use the knife. It didn't cause this. A Traveler willingly gave their life to create that knife, just like I did to have you."

Betha tried to find the right words. "I love you so much, and it hurts."

"I always knew I would die young, but every single moment I had with you was worth it. I love you. You will shine as the brightest of us." Her mother looked over her shoulder and gave a nod. "When you see your father, tell him I forgive him, and it's time for him to move on." With that, Josephine faded.

"Father? Mom—don't go!" The fireflies flew away from her mother's form, and Betha could see through her.

"I love you, my daughter."

Then Betha was alone under the moon, the knife glowing brightly.

TONI'S NOTES

I hope you enjoyed getting to know Betha and the gang in Choice of the Traveler! Let your friends know what you think of the book. If you leave a review of the book, send it to me: toni@tonibinns.com! I love to read reviews and feature them on my social media sites.

These characters have been inside my head for several years begging to be let out into the world. Now, I have the chance to share them and it is an amazing feeling. Choice of the Traveler serves as an introduction to the Nexus Universe. All of these stories will be set in these worlds connected to the Nexus. So you will see familiar faces popping into different books. The lore I'm building is rich and deep, as you can see already, and this is only the beginning of the journey!

Next up is Call of the Traveler and we get to leave Terra for a much longer stint. I can't wait to hear what you think of the wider worlds we will get to travel within.

To stay up to date join my newsletter: tonibinns.com

For book snippets, quotes and artwork check out my Instagram: @tonibinnsauthor

Milton Keynes UK
Ingram Content Group UK Ltd.
UKHW040704201123
432908UK00001B/75

9 798985 307306